WHEELS FOR CONQUEST

BY HARRIETT H. CARR

Where the Turnpike Starts
Against the Wind
Miami Towers
Wheels for Conquest

BY HARRIETT H. CARR

WHEELS for CONQUEST

The Macmillan Company
New York, 1957

Library of Congress catalog card number: 57-5968

First Printing

PRINTED IN THE UNITED STATES OF AMERICA

WHEELS FOR CONQUEST

U. S. 966259

1

KINGS OF THE ROAD

George Bauman sang lustily and the blue hills of Pennsylvania echoed the words and the ringing notes. His voice was a deep bass now, strong with the power of young manhood. George was seventeen.

He rode on the white oak lazy-board which protruded from the bottom of his father's huge Conestoga wagon. The body of the wagon was blue, the wheels and running gear vermillion, and the top of heavy white homespun, a gay splash of color against the November landscape. On the level stretches George would sit astride Bill, the wheel horse. Always the left-hand, heavy side horse next to the wagon was the wheel horse and the drivers rode them only, but here in the hill country George must be on the lazy-board to manage the brake lever.

> "Yesterday Michael dropped around,
> Frederick Michael dropped around," he sang.

It was an old schnitzing party song and it made George think of Anna Showalter and her bobbing, corn-yellow curls that the boys loved to pull. Teasing didn't bother Anna. She laughed and ran away.

George sang happily. In celebration of his first trip to Pittsburgh as a farmer, or "militia" wagoner, Anna had made the bright red tassels that hung from the bridles of his six bay Conestoga horses. She had made them for his half-brother, Johannes, too, who was driving just ahead of him.

> "He reached right down to his girl friend's toe
> And asked her 'What is this?'
> 'This is my pretty little toe
> That I must carry wherever I go. . . .' "

The song ended abruptly, for George had seen something alarming. Ahead, the lead horses were starting on an up-grade, while the wagon was still on the down-grade of the hill it had not quite descended. In another second, the wagon tongue would ram into the rocky hillside. He knew it could break, upsetting the wagon and spilling the load of manufactured goods he was hauling to Pittsburgh. The horses might even be injured!

One horrified glance measured the distance between the two hills. It was shorter than the length of the three teams and the fourteen-foot-long wagon, a stretch of about sixty feet, all told.

George had no time to think. The uneven roadbed on the up-grade sloped sharply downward to the left. That was his only hope . . . his only salvation from an accident.

"Haw! Haw!" He pulled on the jerk-line that guided Barney, the lead horse. His Louden whip sang over the broad rumps of the middle team. The end of the wagon tongue was held up by their harness straps.

"Up with you! Haw!"

The bays learned the sting of a whip. Big Sall lifted her head and the wagon tongue rose with it. Up! Higher! The whip sang over Sall's back again. One inch of clearance would be enough. One inch, liewer Gott! . . .

Iron-shod hooves rang against road stones. Heaving animals snorted and puffed and pulled at the six-ton load. An axle creaked under the strain. Harness bells rang jerkily.

"Up with you! Haw!"

They pulled to the left, responsive to Barney's guidance. The wagon tongue passed above the rut, grazing disaster by a hair's breadth.

"Gid-dap! Gid-dap!"

No time to stop. No time for anything but reaching the top. The high rear wheels were on the level stretch at the bottom now, and George released the brake. The front wheels began inching forward on the uphill crawl. Trouble, of a kind no wagoner should have, had been averted by the lunge of Big Sall and the space between wagon tongue and rocky up-grade. George had managed his team and his load!

At the summit he stopped the panting horses and wiped the sweat from his forehead with a mitten-covered hand. Even his dog seemed to have sensed their close escape. Tawny, shaggy Wasser was trembling on his haunches, crouched near the heavily-loaded wagon, the usual friendly barking silenced.

One thought crowded all else from George's mind. Why hadn't Johannes warned him of this?

George listened. Safely past the treacherous "V" in the road, perhaps a quarter of a mile ahead, he could hear the faint chorus of the bells that decorated the hames of all their horses except the saddle horse on each wagon. Johannes was driving his own wagon—the wagon their father had given him when he became eighteen. George was driving one of the new wagons he had helped to make in his father's shop. It was not his own, but he did not resent that. Johannes was the elder son, two years older than George.

But Johannes had been wagoning for two winters and he knew the road. Had he wanted George to meet with an accident, so he could come to the rescue and claim the bells that hung from the hames of the bays? That was tradition with the wagoners on the Conestoga Road from Philadelphia to Pittsburgh in 1817, and they both knew it. Johannes had played him a trick that called for retribution! He must be listening now for the shout that would have brought him back to help. Well, there would be no shout. As soon as he could get his breath, as soon as his heart slowed back to normal, George would sing again! He would sing until the hills thundered with the echoing!

George looked back at the rock-filled, rutted, defiant road, wondering what new dangers lay ahead. He got his grease box down. The complaining axle must have attention. Then, over the hill behind him came another wagoner's team and involuntarily George called out:

"Wait! Don't go down!"

The wagoner had been riding his wheel horse. He stopped at the brow of the hill and looked ahead to George.

"Ya, I know," he called. Then he unhitched his two lead horses, tied them near the tool box at the right side of the wagon, and climbed his lazy-board to manage the brake.

"Move ahead," he shouted. "I'll need room at the top, where you are."

Clearly this wagoner had been over the road before and knew how to manage. The narrow space between the two hills was about the length of his wagon and two teams of horses. The lead team would be hitched to the load again after the wagon was safely down and the middle team ready to move up the incline. He had an extra horse, too, tied behind his wagon. Seeing it, George knew him to be a "regular" wagoner, who had no other occupation.

George drove ahead a short distance, then stopped and greased his axle while his team rested and he waited for the driver to reach the top. Were there more danger spots along the Conestoga Road that Johannes had not warned him about? Perhaps this man would tell him.

He must make amends to Sall, too, for lashing at her. It was her instant response to the pull of Barney, the lead horse, and the unexpected sting of the whip, that had saved them. He took an apple from his pocket, broke it into two parts with a quick twist and offered it to Sall. His hand on her moist neck was firm and he patted her shoulder kindly.

"Good Sall!"

The horse looked at him with uncertain eyes, and sniffed the pungent apple. She nuzzled his arm while he stroked her side and talked to her reassuringly. Wasser rubbed against his legs, claiming attention.

At last the stranger pulled his sweating, panting horses to a halt just behind George. He was a man in his thirties, George judged, and getting stout. It was difficult to tell the color of his hair for the high-crowned, broad-brimmed felt hat was pulled well down on his forehead, but his face was the face of a reliable Pennsylvania Dutchman and his gray eyes were friendly.

"You made that hill without unhitchin'?" he asked in disbelief. "You never done this trip before?"

He was taking George in—seeing blond hair curling now with sweat, steady blue eyes, honest, well-rounded features.

"Never before," George admitted. Then, "My name is Bauman. George Conrad Bauman."

"Weller," the man introduced himself. "Peter Weller."

"Is there more like this ahead yet?" George asked.

Weller shook his head. "One's a-plenty. But there's Indian bridges I never take. Nothin' but trees layin' across creeks, and hacked down to make a flat road bed. Only it ain't flat. Drive your horses through the water. It cools their feet and the wagon wheels too. I'll be right behind you to give you the signal. Didn't nobody tell you about this road?"

George thought before he answered. He was ashamed to tell the truth, but Weller was sure to learn it when they overtook Johannes tonight. He would thrash Johannes this time for playing him such a trick.

It had been years since they last fought. Not since they were in school, when Johannes, thinner but with longer legs and arms, had been able to win. After George had overtaken Johannes in size they had never fought. George would not have wanted his older brother to get a beating from him, in front of everyone in the neighborhood, and for three years at least George had been sure he could beat Johannes. But this was different. George had come into his own bull-strength and Johannes had asked to learn it, this night.

"I should have been warned but wasn't," George finally admitted.

Weller was still looking him over, and taking in the build of his sturdy horses, the workmanship on the wagon. George was proud of the wagons he had helped his father build. Proud of the handsome iron work on this one, designed like fern leaves. Gideon Hefs, the apprentice iron worker, had forged it in Shtuffle Henning's blacksmith shop, and Gid was George's friend. This winter Gid would forge the iron for George's own wagon. The wood was seasoning now.

"My father is Jacob Bauman," George told Weller. "Have you heard of him? He's been a wagonmaker back in the Conestoga Valley for twenty-five years now."

"And a good one, I see," Weller observed. He was looking from the solid end gate to the hook and link in the chains that kept the boat-shaped wagon bed from spreading. He took his hat off to wipe dirt and sweat from his forehead and George saw he was quite bald. It made him look older.

"So?" the driver asked. It was time to move on.

George looked at the road ahead. For a stretch it was level, then it twisted around a hill. Better be safe and ride the lazy-board again, ready to work the brake if he came upon another dip. He called to his horses.

"Gid-dap!"

Wasser ran and barked gleefully. Iron tires rattled over stones and ruts, harness bells chimed reassuringly. George Bauman would get to Pittsburgh and back with his bells on no matter what lay ahead!

> "If the jug has a hole in it,
> Liewer Heinrich, liewer Heinrich?"

Peter Weller sang the verses and George gave the response.

> "Stupid thing, then plug it up."

The verses were endless. They sang around the rutted bends, through the creeks, over the rude bridges and past the log-house inns that lined the road.

> "Yeah! What should I plug it up with,
> Liewer Heinrich, liewer Heinrich?"
> "Stupid ox, with some straw."

The air was crisp and clear, the hillsides green with pines and brown with bare branches of hickory and oak and chestnut. In his pocket George carried a handful of shining brown nuts from the chestnut trees in his own home yard. It was an old superstition that chestnuts would ward off rheumatism and other ills and bring luck on the road, and his mother had handed them to him before he started.

"Mem, I'd not get rheumatism!" George had scoffed.

"Now you take them and don't be so smart," she had said, pushing them into his pocket. She was a small woman and the work she did from daylight until long after candles were lit, feeding and clothing a man and five children, had kept her much less round than her husband.

"John?" she had asked next, taking care to call her stepson by the English name he preferred. Johannes' own mother had been the daughter of an Englishman and he seemed to be proud and superior because of it.

George could see Mem now, her soft gray hair in a small knot at the back of her head, her blue eyes looking at Johannes hopefully, and her hand extended with the chestnuts. Johannes had taken them and stuffed them into his pocket without a word. Whatever his faults, he had never been gruff with Mem, but he had not shown her much love, either.

Feeling proud and superior was his trouble, George thought, his eyes on the swaying bay rumps. Johannes had never made a friend of Gid, either. Gid's father had died when he was only ten, and his mother had turned her son over to the blacksmith as soon as Gid was big enough to lift a hammer. Then she had married again and left the valley, but Shtuffle Henning and his wife had been kinder to Gid than his own parents, and no one had any reason to either pity or look down on the apprentice.

Nor did anyone, unless it was Johannes. Johannes had been looking more and more at Elizabeth Yoder at the schnitzing parties and husking bees. Old August Yoder, her father, was the richest man in their valley and he felt superior too, but for all that, George had an idea Pep might have planned a marriage for Johannes with Elizabeth, just as he had always been sure

Pep and Mr. Showalter intended he and Anna would marry. Well, let Johannes have Elizabeth and all she would inherit! Tonight Johannes was to learn a lesson.

George hurried the bays along at the thought of it. They should cover fourteen miles today. Johannes might be planning to get ahead of him. There were inns every mile at least, and if Johannes gained even one mile they might not meet again until they got to Pittsburgh. George would not dare move his load over the uncertain road after dusk.

There was scarcely time to go on to another inn when George slowed his team to a crawl at the Sign of the Black Bear. The inn yard was filled with wagons and teams, and he looked quickly from one to another. He would know his brother's wagon anywhere. Wasn't he the one who had helped build it? Johannes was no hand at wagon making.

From a hill behind the sprawling log barns came excited shouts and cheering. A boasting challenge, derisive ridicule. The snatches that came to George were well punctuated with profanity.

This was not George's first night on the road and the rough language of the wagoners, so in contrast with his father's slow talk and deeply religious thinking, was no surprise to him now. He had heard their tall tales nightly and seen the tests of strength they engaged in for amusement. Something of the kind was going on at the hill behind the barn.

"This looks like it for tonight," Peter Weller called to him.

George glanced at the rose-tinted sky ahead. Yes, the Black Bear would have to be their stopping point. Night came quickly in the hills in November.

He drove into the yard, lining his wagon parallel to the road for easy leave-taking in the morning. Weller drove alongside, and a stable boy came from the barns to see whether they were "regulars" who needed feed for the animals or "militia" who carried their own grain and would want only shelter for the horses. The stable boy showed Weller a deference not accorded George.

"Contest on?" Weller asked.

"Same as every night," came the answer. "Tonight Big Lou Ludwig's got a fool militiaman to wager his team can outhawl Lou's."

The stable boy made no secret of his low opinion of the drivers from the farms, but that no longer troubled George.

"Big Lou?" Weller asked with interest. "We must see this."

Then George spied Johannes' wagon, well to the far side of the yard and as near out of sight from the road as could be. His cheeks burned at the sight. Had Johannes placed it there with a purpose in mind—that it should not be seen from the road? He must have hoped George would go past the Black Bear tonight.

George brought the heavy feed trough from the rear end gate and secured it to the wagon tongue. He slammed the projecting iron bar into the staple on the tongue with all his force, indignation mounting. He would feed his horses before he sought out Johannes. They had earned a good portion of grain. He started next to the barns to look over the accommodations. Not all barns were kept clean by the stable boys and oftener than not he had pitched out manure and laid fresh straw for his bays before he took them inside for the night.

Weller, however, was anxious to see what contest might be going on.

"The Black Bear's barns is all right, George," he said. "Come on. Big Lou's the most powerful man on the road. Once I seen him stand up under a half-ton of pig iron that had been loaded on his back, and walk away with it."

There was grudging admiration in his voice.

Half a ton of pig iron! George wasn't sure he believed any man could stand up under such a load, let alone walk away with it. This likely enough was another of the tall tales he had been hearing every night. George didn't question it, though. He was fortunate to have a recognized regular as his companion and friend.

Shouting men and barking dogs led them unerringly to the hill beyond the trees that banked the barn. At the clearing George stopped aghast. Two teams and two drivers were lined up, preparing for a test of strength.

Big Lou and Johannes!

Six powerful chestnuts and six dappled grays, and the chestnuts were being guided to a massive wagon loaded with iron by a man no less commanding. In the fading light George could not see his features, but he hulked above Johannes, a giant oak beside a seedling.

"Look at them chestnuts," Weller was saying. "Fine Conestoga horses, standing seventeen hands high and weighing eighteen hundred each."

George did not answer. He, too, stared at the powerful chests, short arched necks, long legs and flat hoofs. But Johannes' grays were no less to be admired. Heads small and well proportioned, hindquarters splendid, bellies tight drawn. Their horseshoes measured nine inches in breadth and more than nine inches in length Gid had told him when they were last shod.

"The grays don't match the chestnuts in weight," George said through teeth that fairly chattered. To himself he added the thought that Big Lou hadn't won yet.

Bets were offered loudly and freely but few were taken for no one wished or dared bet against Lou Ludwig. Johannes alone would wager a levy on the shining grays. He was facing more than a contest. Derision and aggravating laughter were all the wagoners had for a militiaman who would be so fool-hardy as to match his team against Ludwig's.

Involuntarily George shuddered as the men jeered Johannes. Never had he seen his half-brother so determined or looking so bitter. His lean face was drawn taut, his brown eyes flashed, and when he tossed his hat aside, the dark hair hung low over his forehead. He was alone against this crowd. Johannes was proud of the dappled grays, George knew, but what pride and folly had goaded him into the competition?

"Show the swine what a real team can haul, Lou!"

"Maybe he can beat you downhill, yet!"

A piece of dung was thrown at the grays and Johannes turned, ready to fight, but a shout went up and a gunshot pierced the night air. It was the signal.

Like an animal, Lou Ludwig leapt onto his wheel horse and his Louden whip sang above the heads of his chestnuts. Their response was instant, timed to the sound of the gun. They had known contests before.

Zing sang the whip and up the hill went the load, Lou Ludwig shouting curses and endearments in the same breath.

"How heavy is the load?" George asked Weller.

"Eight tons."

George felt as though an iron collar was choking him. Eight tons! It was too much to ask even of these great animals.

The man with the gun was timing the contestants. A cheer went up when Ludwig turned his team around at the top of the incline and drove the wagon back into place at the foot of the hill. He unhitched his horses and gestured to Johannes, as though the race was actually over.

But the excitement-hungry men must watch the kill. They stood on either side of the wagon while Johannes hitched the grays to the load, while he walked from the great wheel horses to the middle team and up to his lead horse. The excitement in the air had affected even the calm Conestogas. Their tails switched and they looked from side to side at the crowd.

Wasser, at George's heels, scented Johannes now and started toward him with an eager yelp. It was all George could do to grab him by a fleeting hind leg and hold him back. This was no time to distract Johannes.

The gun sounded. Johannes leapt to the back of his saddle horse, but the grays did not respond with the instantaneous forward lunge which had given the chestnuts their advantage. The whip sang, Johannes shouted, and the horses started up the hill. Strong necks arched, shoulder and leg muscles flexed and strained, and the load moved forward—steadily and surely to the top. The grays were no less powerful but they had not been as quick at the sound of the gun. George knew, and Johannes must have known, the race had been decided in those first few seconds.

Lou Ludwig and his irruptive admirers ran halfway up the hill to meet their defeated victim, shouting and laughing. They hauled Johannes from his horse and tossed him into the mud at the side of the hill.

"Back to your manure pile, farmer."

"Throw him in the pigsty, yet!"

They were pushing at Johannes, shoving and laughing and cursing in good-natured jest, now that the regular had won. George sensed, as Johannes so obviously did not, that the men were just having their fun. It would soon be over and forgotten. To Johannes, however, it was no joke. His fists lashed out and he kicked at his tormenters, his thin legs lashing at empty air.

George could stand it no longer. He loosened his hold on Wasser's neck.

"Go to Johannes!"

The dog raced ahead, barking wildly, to take his place beside Johannes.

George turned to the driverless, defeated grays. He would unharness them and feed them. He would say nothing. This was no time to square accounts.

"So that's how it is," he heard Peter Weller saying. The man was looking from Johannes to George.

"That's how," George replied and the words came from deep in his throat. He turned away.

Above the laughter and the joking Peter Weller's next words were authoritative.

"Johannes Bauman! I'll top any offer for your grays!"

The laughter quieted and in the unexpected hush George knew that Peter Weller, like Big Lou Ludwig, was a king of the road.

2

STAGE COACH TAVERN

Wrapped in their blankets, lying on their mattresses of straw, George and Johannes slept on the barroom floor that night with the other wagoners. They lay as far apart as possible and neither had anything to say to the other.

The room was hot from the fire in a huge iron stove, heavy with rank tobacco smoke and the odor of unwashed feet, when the talk and singing ended and one by one the men stretched out. It was cold before morning. George shivvered while he carried his bedding back to the wagon and went to the barn to take the bays out for food and water. He was ready to eat when the breakfast bell rang at five o'clock.

The re-kindled fire had warmed the big room of the inn again and the tables were loaded with food. Roast chicken from the night before, pork, scrapple, bread and butter, apple butter and four or five kinds of pie. Wagoners ate but two meals a day, night and morning, and the meals at the inns were almost always the same, but there was more than a man could eat and scraps for Wasser and the other dogs that served as night watchmen for the loads.

George was among the first to leave the Black Bear. Johannes would be near the last for his wagon was farthest from the road. Other drivers would have to get out of the yard ahead of him. If he guessed right, George would see no more of Johannes until they reached Pittsburgh. But no matter. The day would come when he and Johannes would reckon up accounts.

"Going to Ramsay's at Pittsburgh?" Peter Weller asked while they hitched their teams and prepared to leave.

"Johannes says he's one who always knows where to get business for the haul back," George replied.

"He does," the wagoner agreed. "Ramsay's a Scotch Irishman with an eye for the Dutch business. We'll get schnitz und knepp that'll beat anything we've had at any inn since Lancaster. Smier case, sauer kraut!" He smacked his lips. "A night's lodging for teams and driver and two meals, includes three drinks at Ramsay's."

He looked at George quickly, apparently recalling that George had not taken part in the roistering that had followed the contest of the night before.

"Would be better if more didn't drink so much," he added.

George wasn't sure who Weller was thinking about. After beating Johannes, Big Lou had insisted they drink together and Johannes had forgotten his humiliation when the talk took a turn in favor of his grays and the strength they had shown.

"Had I been quicker at the start," Johannes had kept insisting last night, and more than one driver began agreeing jovially that the contest had been near a tie. But quiet Johannes was not really one with that noisy boisterous group, try as he might to join their revelry. His face was thin and studious, his mouth sensitive. He had always gone his own way, more often alone than not.

Beyond Harrisburg George met the road crew that was building an improved pike. On the new road toll must be paid, but progress was more rapid and there were fewer hazards. Near Pittsburgh the road was crowded with rigs of farmers taking produce to market, carriages of the gentry, and stage coaches that passed the slow-moving wagons with a great clatter, the drivers shouting for their share of the road while their horses galloped past.

George had been left behind by Weller before they reached Pittsburgh. The regular wagoners often drove seven days a week, but George and Johannes had promised their father not to move their loads on the Sabbath, and while Johannes kept well behind George so they did not stop at the same inn again, George was sure Johannes, too, must be keeping his promise.

George had no thought of not giving road the morning before he got to Pittsburgh when he heard the clang of hooves behind him, the rattle of tires on stones, and the call of the driver. It had rained the night before, a cold rain that had frozen and made the road hazardous. Now sleet and snow whipped the sky and filled the clearing ahead, until the outlines of the roadway were barely visible.

George pulled on the lead line and the bays moved to the left. The stage driver blew his horn, his whip whistled, and with bang and clatter the coach started to pass. The horses were about even with George when the iron tires slid on the ice.

"Whoa! Whoa!" the driver shouted while George watched the horses scramble to keep their footing and his own team pulled farther to the left, out of their way. In seconds, however, the coach lay on its side against a high, over-hanging hillside, the horses pawing and snorting and dragging it along to still greater damage or destruction.

"Whoa! Whoa! Stop, you fools!"

The driver leaped clear of the overturned vehicle. He jerked at the reins and shouted.

"Hey, you! Give a hand!" he called to George. "Don't sit there like an ox!"

"Driver! Help!" came the voices from the coach. "What's happened?"

"Are we all to be killed?"

Cries and shouts of the passengers, stomping and neighing of the horses, and curses of the driver all seemed directed against George. Wasser, racing and barking around the over-turned stage, added to the noise and confusion. George stopped the bays and jumped from his wheel horse prepared to give help, but the volley of abuse stopped him in his tracks.

"Stupid jackass! Why didn't you give way?" the driver de-manded.

"Give way?" George repeated indignantly. "Look where my wagon stands."

George had given more than half the road and there was no disputing it. Meantime the coach door, high in the air now, had been opened by the badly shaken and frightened passen-gers. They crowded and clamored to get out and at last did manage, with precarious footing at the coach door, to jump to the snow-covered road.

First to get out was a tall, thin man who turned his attention at once to helping the others, most of whom were all too ready to shout angrily at George as soon as their feet met earth again. George was about to mount his horse and drive off, leaving the lot of them to right the coach as best they might, when the thin man turned on his companions.

"Look at the road and you'll see the man gave full half and more," he said scarcely glancing at George. Then he sneezed and pulled the collar of his greatcoat up around his neck. It was a garment of finer material than George had ever seen—much more elegant than the coarse linsey coat he wore over his leather trousers and jacket. George wondered if it could be as warm, even with the hand-knit scarf which the man was wrapping around his chin and ears, and the big beaver hat which surely had been made back in Reading.

Nine men had been riding in the coach. Now all but this one man began to tell the driver how to get the vehicle back on the road, reaching for the wheels and trying to pull them down to earth.

"You'll pull the wheels off if you don't take care," George cautioned. They were going about the task in the wrong way altogether.

Once more the thin man sneezed. He walked quickly from the coach to the wind-break afforded by the big bays as though hoping to share the warmth of their bodies. His shoulders were shaking with cold.

"They don't deserve it, but I'd be obliged if you'd tell the driver how to get that disgraceful vehicle he calls a stagecoach back on the road," he said to George. "I doubt if he knows how, and I'm sure his passengers don't. A few more jerks and the thing will fall apart altogether."

He spoke impetuously, but with respect for George's knowledge of four-wheeled vehicles and his evident strength.

George crossed the road and sought out the driver. He turned out to be better versed in the management of his outfit than his passengers had given him credit for. George's sturdy shoulder, added to the pushing and shoving of the others, finally got all four wheels back on the road.

George disregarded the few grudging words of thanks and turned back to his load. The man was still standing beside the quiet bays, but he was looking at the wagon top, billowing in the wind but securely fastened to the sideboards. His dark eyes were watering with cold and he appeared really sick. Looking at him more carefully, George judged him to be in his late thirties.

"Did you ever see such a disreputable vehicle?" he asked, nodding in the direction of the coach. "The door doesn't close tight. Snow seeps in between the leather side curtains. No protection at all. My seat is right beneath one of the biggest gaps and I've been getting the worst of it all the way from Harrisburg. Do you think one of the lot would offer to change places with me? Not that I blame them."

It was, indeed, a second-rate coach and not brilliant with gilt and paint as some George had seen on the road, nor well put together.

George thought of his mattress and blankets, safely stowed away under the sturdy white top of the wagon. No snow and little wind could get in there. He wondered if the gentry knew how wagoners traveled. Would he dare propose his simple comforts to a man of such obvious dignity and wealth? George hesitated. The least he could do was offer. Pep and Mem never failed in their hospitality to strangers.

"You're welcome to crawl inside and wrap yourself in my warm bedding," he said at last. "The wagon will be slower, and rough too," he warned.

"No rougher than that rattletrap," the stage passenger said. "If you'd accommodate me as far as the Big Sorrel Tavern I can get a rig there and . . ."

Once more he sneezed.

Eight rounded bows held the heavy, tightly-woven homespun top over George's wagon. He opened the end flap at the front and the coach passenger climbed into the shelter. He was agile and not unacquainted with wagons. Unhesitatingly his feet found the wagon tongue, and his hands gripped at the sideboards.

"We should be at the Big Sorrel by noon," he called down. Then, with another sneeze, dropped the flap and George made it secure from the outside.

George hoped he would recognize the Big Sorrel when he came to it. Actually he had no trouble for the tavern was a huge, two-story building of brick and stone, its name painted in dark red letters on a heavy sign that rocked in the wind and snow above the watering trough. George knew at once it was not a wagoners' inn, but when he roused his passenger the man insisted that George tie his horses to the rum strap and come in for a warm meal before going farther.

"Who knows but I may have to accept your hospitality all the way to Pittsburgh?" he commented. "By the way, we should at least know each other's names. I'm William Wilkins."

"I'm George Bauman and I come from Lancaster way, in the Conestoga Valley," George said. "You're welcome to ride with me, but if I judge right I'll not be welcome at the Big Sorrel."

George was well aware of his rough appearance. He had been two weeks on the road with no chance to do more than comb his hair and wash his hands and face. It was well that his mother, with her "crazy-clean" ways, did not know of conditions in the wagoners' inns. Johannes had never said much about them.

Mr. Wilkins, however, insisted. "You'll be my guest and if the Big Sorrel doesn't like both of us, we'll take our business elsewhere. Tie your horses and come with me, George. I know the host well."

The innkeeper greeted Mr. Wilkins warmly and seeing that George was with him, motioned both to a table near the fireplace where a blazing log of white oak sparkled and smoked and sent its cheering warmth to welcome them. There were half a dozen men at tables eating and drinking. All spoke to

Mr. Wilkins as soon as he came in. The man stood with his back to the fire and fumbled in his pockets for a handkerchief.

George wished it had been possible for him to change into the clean clothes his mother had provided for both himself and Johannes when they started. He remembered his father's admonition to speak English when he reached the city instead of the mixture of Dutch and English spoken at home. It was a good thing, he thought now, that his father had married an English woman and learned the ways of the gentry from her; that in Germany he had gone to school and was convinced of the value of an education. He had insisted his boys stay in the village school longer than any others in the neighborhood.

The men in the inn paid little attention to George. They began plying Mr. Wilkins with questions, giving George an opportunity to look about him. The big room had a different atmosphere from the wagoners' inns. Behind a latticed enclosure the innkeeper sat on a high stool, a king on his throne. A stairway led to a floor above where George judged overnight guests slept in beds, and not on the bare floor.

Crossed guns, stuffed owl and deer heads decorated the walls, and over the fireplace the head and neck of a great sorrel horse looked down.

A barmaid brought steaming plates of chicken and dumplings, hot bread and honey in the comb, and George's attention was drawn from the room to the meal before him. He began to listen to the men who were still questioning Mr. Wilkins.

"When do you figure the road can be completed?"

"Will it furnish a good thoroughfare, linking with the old Philadelphia-Lancaster Road?"

"It will be a year before it's done," Wilkins answered taking a steaming drink the innkeeper himself brought. "It will be a better road than the National Pike."

One of the Big Sorrel guests, older and more sour looking than the others, banged his mug on the table. "Damn Henry Clay! Damn Uriah Tracy!"

George had heard of Henry Clay but not Uriah Tracy. He wondered what these men had to do with the Pennsylvania road and the National Pike, and he looked at Mr. Wilkins hoping for an answer.

"Clay and Tracy—Tracy's from Connecticut—outsmarted us in Congress," Mr. Wilkins explained as though he knew the question George hesitated to voice. "Back in 1806 when the law authorizing a National Pike was passed, they got the route to end in Wheeling, in spite of all we could do to have it run to Pittsburgh or Steubenville."

"When will the Pike be finished?" the embittered man asked.

"From what we hear it will be 1818, about the same time as we get our road through," Mr. Wilkins said. "They're having more trouble than we had, what with Congress not appropriating funds and everyone trying to make a piece of money out of it."

"Ours is a toll road, don't forget," Mr. Wilkins was reminded. "With a free road running from Baltimore to Wheeling, it'll be hard on Pennsylvania. All the immigrants and freight are sure to be diverted."

Mr. Wilkins nodded soberly. "Pittsburgh already has felt the sting," he admitted. "Employment in our industries is lower than a year ago. It worries me. When the road is through to Wheeling the keel boats and barges coming up from New Orleans will leave their loads there instead of coming on up the Ohio to dock at our wharves."

George began to wonder for the first time about this National Pike and about Pittsburgh, too. He had always thought of it as a great city, "Gateway to the West." Now here these men from Pittsburgh sat, talking as though the city was doomed.

"We'll get better men in Harrisburg and in the United States Senate another year," one of the Tavern guests said emphatically. "Now if you'd been there, Wilkins..."

George looked at the man across the table with new interest and not a little awe. From the first he had recognized Mr. Wilkins as a person of superior bearing. Now it appeared he was a man of more than ordinary prestige.

If Mem could see him now. And Johannes! Johannes would have given his lead horse to have supped with men like these ... to converse with Mr. Wilkins.

The conversation turned from roads and politics as abruptly as it had begun.

"Have any of you got room for a passenger to Pittsburgh?" Mr. Wilkins asked turning from his table to the men in the room. "My friend George can take me the rest of the way I guess, but I should be back at my business as soon as possible."

Several voices answered. There would be a way for Mr. Wilkins to get back to the city more fitting to his station in life than the top of a loaded Conestoga wagon.

The innkeeper offered more food and Mr. Wilkins urged George to have his fill.

"Another mile in that wretched coach and I'd have died of pneumonia," he said. "When you get to Pittsburgh I want you to look me up. Perhaps I can show you more of the city than you'd see otherwise. You'll find me at the Bank of Pittsburgh."

"The Bank. ..."

George had never been inside a bank in his life.

"Have you a load to take back to the seaboard?" Mr. Wilkins asked.

"No, but I expected to get one through Ramsay, who has an inn and a ferry...."

"I know," Mr. Wilkins interrupted. "He does well with the wagoners and by them, too. But look me up tomorrow. The bank knows about business, also."

Mr. Wilkins had finished eating and the barmaid was removing the dishes. George knew he should be on his way. He took the hand his new friend extended with a surge of excitement and no little anxiety, too. The Bank of Pittsburgh!

"I'll see you then? For a surety?"

"You'll see me," George promised.

3

TALL TALES AND RED CURLS

The snow flurry ended and the sun came out while George dined at the Big Sorrel. Now the air was clear. Woodpeckers drilled at the trees along the road, a sharp drumbeat to accompany the bell notes from the horses' hames. George hurried them along. He had lost two hours' time or more, what with the upset stage and the stop at the tavern. He must reach Ramsay's inn before dark.

Never did George forget his first glimpse of Pittsburgh. Throughout the afternoon he had been conscious of increasing confusion on the road. There were more rigs and of greater variety; more men calling to horses and to each other. The wild countryside had given way first to neat farm houses, then to a profusion of rough shacks and small log cabins, and the deer and red fox no longer were seen racing into the woodlands. He was conscious, too, of a heavy haze ahead like the smoke of many fires rising from the foot of the hills lining one side of the road. They stretched ahead, rock layer piled on jutting rock layer, four hundred or even six hundred feet high. There was a sound, too, like the rushing of wind through a forest—and then the Monongahela.

The winter sunset gilded the broad waters flowing from the south that would join the Allegheny from the north to form the surging headwaters of the great Ohio. Tomorrow George would see that sight which he had pictured in his mind for a long time. Tomorrow he would see the whole city of Pittsburgh. Looking ahead he realized the haze he had been observing was indeed smoke; smoke rising from hundreds of chimneys and funnelled upward by the surrounding hills. He had heard of Pittsburgh's smoke before, but had forgotten.

The yard of Ramsay's inn was crowded to overflowing with teams and wagons when he got there but even in the hubbub and fading light George had no difficulty in spotting Johannes' outfit. While he was at the Big Sorrel his brother had gone on ahead of him. He wondered what mood Johannes would be in tonight. He could not have failed to see the bays tied to the post at the stage coach tavern, a place wagoners did not frequent. The passing of the days had dulled the sharp edge of George's anger, but how would he find Johannes?

A stable boy interrupted George's thoughts.

"No room for your teams inside," he called. "More'n one driver will sleep in his wagon tonight." Then he turned abruptly from George to resume his work.

"Are there accommodations anywhere else?" George inquired. "This night will not be pleasant for man or beast, outside."

"Some went on to the Green Tree but come back. They're

full, too. Outside at Ramsay's is better'n inside at the Green Tree."

The stable boy was looking at George's outfit, sizing up his teams and wagons.

"Drive yore wagon onto them planks ahead or it'll be froze into the ground come mornin'," he directed. "A wagon like yurn'll sink to the axles if it stands long in this here mud, and all the space that's cobblestoned is took already."

George was sure he was right. Wagons were crowded together on the section of the yard that had been paved. He drove cautiously until the wheels were secure on the planks which had been provided for emergencies such as this. Then he unhitched, took his axe from the tool box, and with two of the horses hurried back to a clump of trees he remembered. While there was still light to do it he must gather a good supply of branches and lay a firm foundation of pine boughs for the horses' hooves, covering it with straw, or the animals' feet would be frozen in the mud too, by morning.

When at last he left his bays, three tied to either side of the wagon tongue, they were as comfortable as he could make them, each animal covered with his "housing" of deerskin. For the first time on the long trip to Pittsburgh they would have to stay outside, and George with them, for no wagoner slept inside while his horses shivered in the cold.

Most of the drivers had finished eating when George forced his way into Ramsay's crowded inn. The room was the largest he had seen anywhere along the road, and a horse had just been driven in through a back door to haul a log for the huge fireplace against the farther wall. A six-foot poker, in the hands of an angular man in shirt sleeves, was forcing the log from the hearth onto the glowing embers.

George looked for Johannes but at first did not see him.

Men were playing whist or loo, singing and clowning, and from a recess near the bar, musicians with violins, accordion and banjo were tuning up. Near the musicians George spied Peter Weller and he made his way toward the table where his friend was sitting. Weller, he soon discovered, was engaged in swapping stories with any who would listen.

"Big?" he heard the wagoner ask. "Why, where I come from. . . ." Weller pounded his mug on the table to attract the attention of a barmaid and went on with his story:

"Why, I was settin' on an old log last spring, eatin' an apple. Jest an ordinary-sized apple about like the pumpkins raised here-abouts. When I finished paring it I stuck my knife in the log and didn't the thing start movin'! A black snake, that's what it was. Not a log at all. I rode the thing all the way from Germantown to Coventry Iron Works."

"That musta been the day of the big wind," another wagoner chimed in. "It took seven men to hold my hat on my head!"

Raucous laughter greeted each story. George laughed too. Then, above the din in the room he heard Johannes' voice:

"It's going to take seven hats to fit one wagoner's head, from what I saw today. A wagoner dining with barristers at the Big Sorrel."

There was banter in Johannes' tone, but more than that. He had been talking to the men and they had not believed him, George was sure. Johannes must have stopped long enough to get some information from the stable boy at the coach tavern. Now a chorus of doubting "yeahs?" was directed at Johannes who was coming toward Weller's table. Johannes actually was in high spirits. The mug he held in his hands was filled with a brew stronger than coffee, George feared.

"Tell us about it, George," Johannes said standing in front

of the table and waving his mug toward the men who were crowding around, eager for news if there was any. A lock of unruly hair lay in a heavy wave over Johannes' forehead and his dark eyes were shining with excitement.

"I stopped at the Big Sorrel, yeah!" George said without getting up. "I'd picked up a gentleman named William Wilkins from an accident on the road and I let him off there. And I got to Pittsburgh with my bells on too, Johannes!"

George was in no mood for joking and his tone sobered Johannes. For a moment George thought he might be questioned, but Johannes turned from the table and signalled to the musicians.

"Auch du liewer Augustin," he began singing and they fell in with the tune. Mugs banged on tables and soon wagoners and barmaids were swinging in a vigorous dance around the room.

Weller shook his head. "A strange one, that," he observed. "You could beat him into sausage meat. Why does he keep asking for it?"

"I don't know. . . . Since we were boys. . . ." George gave up.

"I knew brothers like that once," Weller began but he didn't finish his story. Instead he looked at George again. "Why?" he asked.

"Because we're only half-brothers I guess," George tried to explain. "It all began when he found out my mother isn't his mother. Mem and Pep didn't tell us and we didn't know until we were told at school."

George remembered the day only too well. "It was as though Johannes felt he'd been cheated or something," he told the wagoner. "What a beating he gave me that day."

Weller, watching Johannes in the dance, seemed to understand. "You could beat him now, but don't do it," he advised.

"Not tonight, anyhow," George agreed. "What I want now

is food. Is that Ramsay? The one who was working the log onto the fire when I came in?"

"Jim Ramsay himself," Weller said. "From the moors of Scotland and the peat bogs of Ulster." Then he shoved his chair away from the heavy table to join the others in the dance. George made his way to the bar.

"I'm told there's no room for my horses, but can I get a meal?" he asked. "I was late getting here."

"Of course, my friend. How could we have overlooked you."

The deep, gravel-rough voice and the accent were completely foreign to George. James Ramsay was a muscular, stoop-shouldered man of about sixty with sandy hair cropped short about his head and a growth of curling beard along his jaws and over his chin. He moved and spoke with a slow, indifferent air as though he was paying little heed to anyone, but George felt that every detail of his appearance and every word he had spoken were known to the innkeeper. His was not the simple, uncluttered mind of the wagoners, nor even the innkeepers George had met on this trip. How would one know what the man was thinking?

"Over here," Ramsay was directing. "There's a table near the kitchen that might not get kicked over while you're eating. Sit back against the wall or you'll get your feet trampled on."

Ramsay opened the door leading to the kitchen. "Jennie!" he called. "Jennie Gilfillan!"

She came into the room on a run, a slender girl of about George's age with clusters of red curls so heavy they seemed greater than the whole weight of her, and green eyes that looked quickly from the innkeeper to the revelers in the room and finally found George, sitting quietly at the table. Apparently no words were needed between the innkeeper and Jennie Gilfillan. One understanding jerk of her head and she turned and closed the kitchen door behind her flying red and brown plaid skirt and the white homespun apron that almost covered it.

Ramsay went back to his bar and the musicians played on, loudly and vigorously. Stomping feet, laughter and singing fairly rocked the room. The full skirts of the sturdy barmaids ballooned as the men swung them off their feet. It was a sight indeed, but fixed in George's mind was the picture of Jennie Gilfillan. Was she really as slender as she seemed? Her waist so tiny, her hair so copper red, her eyes like green water sparkling in the sun?

She was back with his supper while he was wondering about her. Pork, sauerkraut, potatoes and sweet-sour cabbage. She did not say a word and George was not one to think quickly of what he might say to her. One more trip from the kitchen and she brought bread and apple butter, pie and coffee, and when he looked at her he found her own eyes upon him, questioning, her lips parted as though she would speak.

"It smells good," George said. "Thank you, Jennie Gilfillan."

She nodded and for just an instant hesitated at the table, then she turned back to the kitchen but as she swung around one of the dancing wagoners caught her and drew her toward the noisy merrymakers.

Jennie Gilfillan was not one of them. She bent like a willow wand, slipped quickly from the encircling arm, and the kitchen door shut behind her before the man knew what had happened.

George looked at Ramsay. His half-closed eyes pretended not to see. In his corner next to the musicians he was cautious, watchful, his face a mask.

George waited after he had finished his meal, hoping Jennie would come to clear the table, but an older woman gathered up the dishes and took them away. In no mood to join the revelers, George left the inn. He might as well see how his horses were faring and curl up in his blankets in the wagon. He would have Wasser to help keep him warm.

He was up on the load, preparing to tie the end flap down when he heard his name called softly.

"George. George Bauman!"

It was a girl's voice and although he could scarcely believe it, he knew it was Jennie Gilfillan. Peering into the darkness below him, he saw the upturned oval of her face, framed by a dark scarf that held her curls close to her small head. She had a bundle in one arm and was carrying a huge stein.

"Jennie!"

Without hesitation she stepped around the wheel horse and onto the wagon tongue, holding the stein up to him, then the bundle. Both were hot to his touch—a soap stone and a mug of milk, steaming and spiced with pepper.

"Jennie, don't go."

He balanced the mug carefully and reached a hand down to her. It was surprising that she took his hand, but she did. In a second she was beside him on the load, and he dropped the wagon covering, shutting out the cold night air.

"How did you know my name?" George asked.

"From Johannes." She spoke in a whisper but the burr of the highlands and the clear ring of Ulster were in her voice, too. "Last year he told us you would come this winter."

"Johannes?" George wondered what his brother might have said.

"Drink your hot milk," Jennie ordered. "It'll warm you through and if you start the night warmed, 'twill not be so bad. Then I'll tell you why I came."

"Whatever the reason, I'm glad you came," George told her

as he raised the warm stein to his lips. Beside him, in the darkness, she was like a firefly in the night.

"It's a favor that maybe you can do for me," Jennie finally explained. Her words and her breath came quickly, as though she could not stay with him long. "Tomorrow morning I think Mr. Ramsay will ask you to take a load to Wheeling before you go back to Philadelphia. If you should decide to go. . . ."

"To Wheeling?"

"To Wheeling," she repeated. "If you decide to go will you inquire there for my father? Robert Gilfillan's the name and he's a trapper."

"I'll inquire," George promised, scarcely realizing what he said.

"Tell him—if you should see him or find any way to get word to him. . . ." She hesitated.

"Yes? What would you have me tell him?"

"Tell him Mrs. Ramsay is dead."

Then she was moving away, reaching for the wagon flap and preparing to leave him. George caught her arm and held her back. He mustn't let her go yet. There was more to this than she was saying. Without the words being spoken, George was sure that Jennie was in trouble or afraid of something.

"Wait," George whispered. "Is something wrong? Is . . . is Ramsay mean to you?"

"No, not mean," Jennie answered. "Not exactly. But my father left me with Mr. and Mrs. Ramsay when my mother died five years ago. He couldn't take a bit of a girl with him into the Ohio country, you know. Mrs. Ramsay mothered me and sent me to school and kept me as if I were her own. But now there's no place for me except. . . ."

George knew what she meant. No place for her except the kitchen of a wagoners' inn.

"He never comes home any more," Jennie explained. "I

mean, to the house where he lived with Mrs. Ramsay. All the time it's business. All the time at the inn, night and day."

George tried to follow her meaning and understand correctly what she was telling him.

"You think he'll ask me to go to Wheeling? Why?"

George had never thought of going beyond Pittsburgh. He had scarcely heard of Wheeling until that day.

"I'm sure he will." Jennie was very positive. "Last year he studied Johannes but didn't ask him. He picks men very carefully. From what Johannes said I was sure he had you in his mind. Tonight I knew." U. S. 966259

Johannes again. "What did Johannes say?" George asked.

"I think Johannes is jealous," Jennie told him. "I think he would have liked to meet up with Mr. Wilkins. I heard what he had to say tonight. Last year he boasted and said you'd be king of the wagoners one day. Mr. Ramsay has been waiting to see if it was just another tall tale, what he said about you. But I know him, and every look that comes into his eyes. If I mistake not, he'll ask you in the morning. And in the morning there'll be no way for me to talk to you."

"If he asks me to go to Wheeling . . ." It puzzled George. What was he to do if such an adventurous proposition was put to him? He tried to think, in the quiet of the wagon where the sound of the horses crunching their grain and Wasser's even breathing were familiar and reassuring.

"I'm not saying you should go," Jennie seemed to sense the question in his mind. "But if you do . . ."

"If I go, you already have my promise."

She raised the wagon flap and a small foot reached downward. George took her by the waist and lowered her carefully to the wagon tongue.

How light she was. And what a load of anxiety and trouble might be weighing on those small shoulders. He handed the empty mug to her and watched while she hurried between the wagons and disappeared in the darkness.

Where was she going? To the inn? To the house where James Ramsay never went any more, now that his wife had died?

4

MACHINES AND MONEYED MEN

The yard of Ramsay's inn was a bedlam in the morning. Wagoners like Weller, who already had loads for Philadelphia, were hurrying to get an early start. Men with merchandise for Pittsburgh were equally eager to get unloaded. Everyone was shouting questions at Ramsay and he was answering with few words, and in no hurry.

"What'll it cost to get a horse shod?"

"Thirty-seven and a half cents."

"What medicine can I give this one? She's sick and getting no better."

"Try three gills of gin and some parsley root in warm milk."

"Who can I see in Pittsburgh to get a load back?"

That was the question George must ask but now he hesitated, remembering what Jennie had told him. For some reason Ramsay had not considered Johannes for the Wheeling trip so George must wait until his brother was out of hearing before he approached the innkeeper. There were things he wanted to know, too, before he undertook such an unexpected venture.

While Johannes was harnessing the grays to deliver his load, George cleaned up and dressed in fresh clothing for he intended to visit Mr. Wilkins at the bank. Finally he sought out Ramsay.

"I've had it in mind to get a load to haul all the way to Philadelphia, not just to Lancaster," George began. "I've never seen the port city. This is my first trip."

Ramsay ignored the last remark. "You can get furs and grain to take back to the coast," he said quietly. "The levee's loaded with bales of cotton and barrels of molasses brought up on the 'Massassip' from New Orleans. Keel boats came in yesterday with cheese and smoked bacon and hams from Ohio and Kentucky, looking for a market. I can tell you who to ask for."

"I'd be obliged to you."

Ramsay's half-closed eyes were taking in the wagons that remained in his yard, and they came to rest on George's strong outfit.

"That one's built to take the toughest roads," he commented. " 'Twill last for generations. If it's new country you'd like to see, and adventure, there's more to be had and for better pay, by taking a load down to Ohio. Or as far as Wheeling, at least."

"I heard Wheeling's destined to get business away from Pittsburgh," George said questioningly. "Is that a proper trip for a Pennsylvania wagoner?"

"Pittsburgh's manufacturing industries have to get their output to market, and the market's Ohio and Kentucky," Ramsay explained. "In the winter, the river's uncertain. Frozen over part of the time. Pennsylvania's roads will save this city's industry. Wilkins must have told you that."

He wasn't looking at George, neither did he ask a direct question, but there was a question in his words, nonetheless. He wanted to know what Wilkins had said, George was sure.

"Mr. Wilkins seeeemed to think the National Pike would hurt this state," George told him, for Mr. Wilkins had made no secret of it. "He was concerned about business. He's an important man here, isn't he?"

Ramsay started walking toward George's wagon.

"He's president of the Greensburgh-Pittsburgh Turnpike Company. President of the Monongahela Bridge Company. President of the Common Council of Pittsburgh. President of the Bank of Pittsburgh."

The recital left George breathless. He, a young wagon-maker from Lancaster way, was to visit this man? Yet Mr. Wilkins had been insistent in the invitation, he recalled.

"You might ask Wilkins what he thinks about taking a load of nails as far as Wheeling, anyway, should you see him."

Then the innkeeper turned away. Plainly he was not going to urge the trip on George.

How did Ramsay know George would see Mr. Wilkins? Or was he merely probing for information? Innkeepers all along the road had been eager for any news the wagoners might bring, but usually they asked openly. Not Ramsay.

George did intend to ask Mr. Wilkins' advice before saying he would go beyond Pittsburgh. No such trip had been in his mind when he left home. Even Jennie's need to get a message to her father was not a sound reason for going he knew, now that he thought of it soberly, in the light of day.

George encountered Mr. Wilkins while he was still thinking of how he should conduct himself when he got to the bank. The man was hurrying along the wooden footwalk, his sharp features contracted and his small mouth closed tightly. It was a strong face, George thought. This tall, rugged man was unlike anyone George had ever known both in looks and bearing. He was abreast of George before he saw him, and he stopped at once with a warm and easy greeting.

"I was just on my way to the levee," Mr. Wilkins said. "Won't you join me? Several river steamers and keels came in yesterday and more this morning. This way."

They started toward the banks of the Monongahela, the direction many people were taking. Ahead of them four or five noisy, roughly dressed men were singing lustily.

"One fine day, one fine day
        A-walking on the quay, a-walking on the quay
    I met a lovely lassy-o
        And with it all so sassy-o
    One fine day!"

It was as wild a song as some the wagoners sang and with as many verses. Mr. Wilkins listened for awhile, apparently in amusement.

"Keel boat men," he explained. "They probably had a night of celebration after their weeks on the river. This way. Look out for the mud."

He stepped gingerly from the footwalk to the rutted street, now crowded with rigs, racing youngsters, barking dogs, and even pigs. With assurance he made his way to the market house on the river bank.

George had never seen such a sight. Men and women haggled and bargained for the homespun linsey-woolsey, the butter and eggs, cheese and smoked meats that had come up from the back country. Others were looking at piles of home-tanned deer and cattle skins. Mr. Wilkins' eyes seemed to take in everything. With a question here, a word there, he was learning what the river men knew of conditions beyond Pittsburgh.

"Come," he said again and led the way out onto the levee.

If Pittsburgh's business had been hurt, the levee that day gave no evidence of it. Men were tossing bags and barrels and bales from the long, slender keel boats which George was sure would carry at least three to four wagon loads of goods—fifteen or twenty tons at least. The flat, majestic river was crowded with boats; stately barges with raised decks, piroques that had been hollowed out from huge trees, and broad Kentucky flats, fifteen feet wide at least and some of them as much as one hundred feet long.

"Look!" Mr. Wilkins directed, pointing to one craft that was having difficulty in moving away from the river bank. It was loaded with household goods, a family, horses and cattle, and crates of chickens. Children were playing with cats and dogs, and an old lady in a rocker, a shawl tight about her shoulders, knitting unconcernedly while the men worked with poles and oars to get their flat boat afloat.

"Will they make it?" George asked.

Mr. Wilkins looked dubious. "They'll probably get clear, but the river's low at this time of year," he said. "It's no time to be setting out, with winter coming on. Pittsburgh to Cincinnati is twelve days at least. Unless the weather holds good, they'll have trouble before they get as far as Wheeling, and they're probably headed for Cincinnati or even Memphis."

"It'll be a hard winter," George told him. "The breast bones of the geese were thick. Onion skins were thick, too."

"Is that how you tell?" Mr. Wilkins asked. "I'd forgotten."

"And by the animals," George explained. "Lots of squirrels came down from the north this fall."

Mr. Wilkins accepted George's harbingers without a sign of questioning.

"Then our friends out there may be cold, in spite of the stove they carry," he said, turning away from the river. "I told you

I'd show you something of Pittsburgh. Before I go to the bank we can take a short walk, if you have time."

"It's you who might not have the time," George suggested.

"To me, this is business," Mr. Wilkins replied. "I rely on my own eyes and ears, not what is told to me, or who knows how badly the bank might be managed. The Bank of Pittsburgh has always paid specie, George, except for one short period during the War."

He spoke with pride.

"You should have seen the city during the War," he went on. "Manufacture was at its height and the factory system developing, to keep up with the demand for things. We've got to get our industries going like that again. Why, this iron foundry we're passing had ten or twelve wagons like yours waiting outside for howitzers and shells to cool, so they could be loaded and taken to Perry at Erie. They made cannon balls here that went down to General Jackson at New Orleans, too."

There were no wagons outside the iron foundry that morning. George wondered what might be manufactured inside, but Mr. Wilkins went on without stopping until he came to a rolling mill.

"This is the sight I had in mind to show you," he said. "Two men, William Stackpole and Ruggles Whiting, have introduced cutting machines that cut and head nails."

No one observed them when Mr. Wilkins opened a door and the two stepped inside. The sight was unbelievable. Nine nailing machines, laid out in a precise row, suddenly burst into rapid motion and with deafening noise. Before his eyes, nails came from these machines—nails which George had supposed only blacksmiths, working with hammers at their forges, could produce and one at a time. It was inconceivable that this could be done. George watched the action of the machines, the majestic swing of the beam, and tried to comprehend but he could not understand the operation. At last Mr. Wilkins turned to the door again and they went outside.

"This factory is one that's not idle, nor laying off workers," Mr. Wilkins said. "A steam engine of seventy horsepower moved the machines you saw."

"Those must be the nails Ramsay said I could take down to Wheeling," George commented as much to himself as to Wilkins. The banker took up the remark at once.

"The nails must travel down to cities in Ohio and Kentucky where there is more building going on than there. During the winter months the best way is by wagon, and old Ebenezer Zane laid out a good route from Pittsburgh to Wheeling, years ago. I've not been over the road recently, but they tell me it isn't bad. Is that what you have in mind?"

"I had it in mind to ask your advice," George said.

"You have a wagon that's new and strong and you're young and strong," Mr. Wilkins observed. "That's what is needed. Men who can manage teams and loads against all hazards. I had an idea Ramsay would be trying to get men for that haul. He's a shrewd man and a wealthy one, with more than one iron in the fire. What's good for Pittsburgh is good for him."

Mr. Wilkins glanced at George before going on. "Did he tell you how many others will be making the trip?"

"No, he didn't say anything about who might be going."

"He knows," Mr. Wilkins said. "Men don't travel that road alone. I should warn you there have been robberies. Are you armed with more than brass knuckles and a black jack?"

Those were the only arms George carried. Robberies were not unknown on the Pennsylvania road, but he had neither seen nor heard mention of a gun.

"In Pennsylvania you'd have no trouble with Indians, but beyond our borders there are roving bands. And within our borders, thieving isn't unknown. On the road to Ohio it's wise to have a Kentucky rifle along. Now don't tell me they're made in Lancaster County," the banker laughed. "My father and his father before him lived there." He took his beaver hat off and rubbed it gently. "I know this comes from Reading, too," he added. "But I also know you won't find sixty-two inns on a sixty-three mile stretch of road, as between Lancaster and Philadelphia. You won't find three thousand wagoners strung along, affording protection to each other, so I'd advise you to go prepared. As a matter of fact, I'd had it in mind to recommend the haul to you, if Ramsay didn't."

"You and Ramsay must be friends," George suggested but the next minute he was sure it was the wrong assumption. Mr. Wilkins frowned but he was not embarrassed by the question.

"Ramsay and I see alike on a lot of things, but not all," he said. "I'm for getting bridges across the Monongahela and the Allegheny, and that'll put an end to his ferry business unless he moves it to some likely point on the Ohio. Then I'm a Federalist and he's a Democrat. I'll never get to the legislature if I have to depend on his vote. But we're both for keeping Pittsburgh as the "Key City to the West" and getting these nails sold is one way of doing it. The Bank of Pittsburgh will extend credit to merchants down river who buy Pittsburgh products."

George and the banker walked in silence for a few minutes watching the panorama of confusion in the business street or glancing down the quieter side streets lined with weeping willows and Lombardy poplars. There were three story buildings ahead of them and George marveled at their height and size.

"There's iron here and our blacksmiths are producing locks and keys and hinges, but the market is farther west," Mr. Wilkins went on. "We have factories that can make grates and shovels and all kinds of heavy farm utensils and tools—all to be taken west. There's a big boat building industry, too. Seven or eight boats are abuilding right now."

George wondered about those factories. Were they equipped with steam-powered engines, too, and laid out with machines in neat rows? He wished he could see more of them.

Gradually, as Mr. Wilkins talked, Pittsburgh's need for an outlet became clear, and the trip to Wheeling, or even farther into Ohio, a thing a man might be proud to do. As for thieving, Indians or white men either, George felt no fear in the bright sunshine of the day and the security of Pittsburgh's Market Street. In the back of his mind, too, there was Jennie Gilfillan. He found himself anxious to return to the inn and talk to Ramsay again about a load to Wheeling, in spite of Mr. Wilkins' warning.

"Mr. Wilkins, I think I'll talk to Ramsay about that load of nails," George said at last. "It would do no harm to inquire, and he's the man to see, isn't he?"

"He can arrange a load for you and it's good for a wagoner to stand in well with him. But you can go direct to Stackpole and Whiting, too."

The banker hesitated at the door of a mercantile house and George surmised he had business inside, but he had one more thing to say.

"If you decide to go," Mr. Wilkins began, his eyes looking back toward the river, "if you decide to go, find out all you can about the National Pike and see me when you return. You'll come upon Mordecai Cochran and his Irish Brigade building the road somewhere in this state, near Uniontown. Make an excuse to talk with the men. Find out when they think they'll get to Wheeling, and listen to all the troubles they've had. They'll be complaining, you may be sure. Keep your ears and eyes open and let me know what you see and hear."

George promised. His mind was all but made up now. He wished Peter Weller had not left that morning for Philadelphia, for he would have liked to talk with a reliable wagoner as well as Wilkins and Ramsay—men with moneyed interests who wanted him to make the trip.

Suddenly George thought of Johannes. Why should he not ask his own brother? For two winters Johannes had been wagoning and never once had he spoken of going beyond Pittsburgh.

And why hadn't Ramsay considered Johannes? Were the dangers of the road so great that a man of Johannes' slight build would find them too rugged? Or were there other reasons? Johannes, for all his impetuousness at times, was no fool. He well might know of conditions which had not been explained to George.

Eagerness for the venture and doubt as to its wisdom were both in his mind while he hurried back to the inn. He would find Johannes there sometime before the day ended, for the horses must have a rest before the return trip started. Johannes would not have re-loaded today and started back so soon. George would forget the incident on the road and see what his brother knew of this Ohio business before he spoke to Ramsay again.

CHAPTER

5

ROAD TO WHEELING

Back at the inn Johannes was grooming his horses, taking great pains to have their manes in smooth waves. George sat down on the wagon tongue and watched the quick, sure strokes. After one brief word of greeting Johannes went on working, his dark eyes intent on the animals. They were getting a thorough going-over. Johannes would make sure they had rested well and were shod and ready for the long haul before he started back, George knew.

"Have you got your load?" George asked at last.

"Molasses for Philadelphia," Johannes answered. He rested one elbow against the supple shoulder of his lead horse then looked down at George. "You?" he asked. "I looked for you this morning but you seemed to know where you were going."

It was surprising, at first, to have Johannes indicate any interest in how George might fare in Pittsburgh. When they started, George had expected his brother to be with him throughout the trip, but Johannes had thrown him entirely on his own to meet the hazards of the road and the nightly contacts and competitions with older and experienced wagoners as best he might. George thought he understood this unexpected gesture of friendliness, however. Like Ramsay, his brother wanted to know what Mr. Wilkins had to say, and like Ramsay, he would not ask.

To retaliate and not talk about Mr. Wilkins was a temptation, but there was nothing to be gained by it. Neither did George want to boast of this new acquaintance as most wagoners would have done, even though he was proud to know a man of importance.

"You know I picked Mr. Wilkins up when his coach overturned in trying to pass me," George said simply. "He invited me to visit him before I left Pittsburgh and I did. I met him, and by accident again, while I was on the way to the bank."

George paused but Johannes asked no questions.

"He recommends that I take a load of nails down to the Ohio market," George went on. "I haven't heard any talk about going to Ohio. What do you think?"

"There're loads going to Ohio regularly and good money for short hauls beyond Wheeling, I've heard." Johannes gave the information almost eagerly. "Are you going to do it?"

"I don't know. From what Mr. Wilkins said there are dangers on the Ohio road."

"None that couldn't happen between here and Lancaster." Johannes looked beyond the muddy inn yard to the towering cliffs and George looked too. There was a wild ruggedness about them, unlike the friendly, rolling hills of the valley at home; a lure of the unknown beyond, and a challenge.

"As a matter of fact, George, I've had it in mind to make that trip myself," Johannes went on, choosing his words carefully. "One of us probably must, and I've thought I should be the one. But it could be you."

George looked at his brother quickly. What was Johannes saying?

"What do you mean, Johannes? Say what you mean."

"Surely you know we can't both stay at home always," Johannes said. "The wagon shop has no room for us both."

Johannes looked at him at last. His eyes were serious, not hostile nor tormenting. Clearly he had been thinking of the years ahead in a way George had not, and George did not follow his reasoning.

"No room . . . ?" George repeated. "Pep has to hire wheelrights. It takes four of us two months to make a wagon, complete with feed box and tar pot and tool kit. You know that."

"I cannot make wagons all my life!"

There was no mistaking the aversion in Johannes' tone, nor disputing what he said. It was George who had studied the wood, learning the difference between white oak and poplar from which the body parts were made, the hickory for axles and gum for hubs. It was George who had learned the use of hand axe, saw and turning lathe. Johannes had never missed an opportunity to get away from the wagonmaker's tasks.

"But there is the farm," George protested, remembering his brother's interests. "The planting and harvest."

"Do you forget the farm belongs to Grandpa Eschleman?" Johannes asked.

It was true that Grossedawdi Eschleman was Mem's father, but he had never treated Johannes differently from the others and the reminder angered George.

"Why must you forever act as though we were two families?" George demanded. "You have worked on the farm more than I and . . ."

But Johannes interrupted.

"It is only sense to recognize facts," he said with finality. "That is why I have thought of seeing what Ohio looks like."

So Johannes had been thinking seriously of leaving home, an idea that had never occurred to George. He could see Pep's face at such news. Johannes was the elder son—his first son. And Mem! She would feel she had failed . . . that it was her fault!

George got up from the wagon tongue. Such a thing could not be.

"On this trip it is I who will go to Ohio," he said. "And think twice before you leave Pep, Johannes."

George did not wait for his brother to answer but hurried across the yard toward the inn. Ramsay would be there, or in the blacksmith shop beyond. He could hear the clang of hammer on iron now. The forge had been alive all night with the business of shoeing horses and making repairs on wagons that were to start at daylight.

George did not let himself hope to see Jennie Gilfillan again, for she had said she could not see him in the morning, but he turned toward the back door of the inn instead of the front entrance. If he stood for a time watching the work at the forge she might see him and make an excuse to come out. Now that his mind was made up he would like to assure her he was going to Wheeling.

It was not necessary for him to make a pretext of watching the blacksmith. When he turned the corner of the kitchen she came out of the door, a heavy wooden pail weighing down one slender shoulder.

"Jennie!"

She stopped, a startled look on her face when she turned toward him.

"Where must this go?" he asked, taking the pail of table scraps from her hand. "Where are the pigs?"

"There. Beyond the forge. I'll go with you."

In the full light of day she was prettier than he remembered her and the sunlight glistened in her hair. The sight of her made George forget his own anxieties and he smiled.

"This is too heavy for you," he said. "It is heavier than you yourself. I'm glad you had to bring it out, though, for it gives me a chance to tell you I'm going to Ohio. I was about to look for Ramsay."

"George Bauman, how glad I am!" Her face lighted with an answering smile. "I thought you would. I hoped and hoped."

"Now you're sure all you want me to tell your father is that one message?" he pressed. "You're sure there isn't more he should know?"

She hesitated, and her reluctance to talk made George certain there was more on her mind.

"If he knows that, he'll understand I should join him in Ohio, if it is possible." Her voice was almost a whisper. "You see, I don't know how he lives there . . . whether he has a house at all . . . whether he spends all his time tramping through the wilderness, trapping and living like an Indian. That's what I've heard wagoners say who've been to Wheeling, but I don't believe most of the wagoners."

"You'd believe me?"

"Yes, I would believe you. I knew it the minute I saw you." Jennie had no hesitancy in saying it and her appraisal pleased George. "When Mr. Ramsay picked you it was because he, too, judged you to be strong and reliable. But I mustn't linger here with you any longer. Empty the pail in the feed trough, quickly George."

"Why? Why must you hurry away?"

George got his answer. The kitchen door opened and a woman's voice, harsh and commanding, called out.

"Jennie! Jennie Gilfillan, come here this minute!"

Jennie reached for the pail but George did not release it at once.

"Please, George." The green eyes were appealing. "It will only make things worse."

George gave her the empty pail but he followed her as she ran quickly to the kitchen. The woman in the doorway was the one who had cleared the dishes from his table the night before and Jennie darted under the arm she held across the entrance as though to block the way against anyone else. She was plump and elderly and she looked at George sharply.

"Jennie Gilfillan ain't for wagoners," she said and turned her back on him.

George thought of those words while he drove his wagon, loaded to capacity with kegs of nails, onto Ramsay's ferry two mornings later. Ramsay might be a hard taskmaster and the woman might be mean, but at least Jennie was safe from the roughness of the drivers and the coarse barmaids who waited on table and joked with the men at Ramsay's inn.

Four wagons were making the trip to Wheeling and as each was ferried across the river the driver waited for the others. The ferry was a flat boat, worked by nine men with poles tipped with iron, so they could break the ice, or if stuck in the muddy river bottom, force the ferry out into the main stream. A tenth man steered with a large oar from behind. They made a noisy business of it, what with grunting and cursing as they pushed the huge load from shore, then singing loudly when they were free in deep water.

Once out of Pittsburgh the road twisted south through rolling, wooded country. Small farms with sheep and cattle about the barns and neat crossroad hamlets had a settled and prosperous look, but there were stretches where George saw nothing but forest. Deer and red fox, bears and even wolves, stared at the clattering wagons or darted into the thickness of the trees at the sound of the bells. He had time now to think again of what Johannes had said and to wonder about the Ohio country.

Was it a farm Johannes had in mind for himself somewhere in this new state, or did he just want to get away from the rest of the family? Particularly, to get away from George? Grosse-dawdi Eschleman's farm was only a short distance down the valley from Pep's wagon shop. Why couldn't Johannes think of that farm as the place for him to work and the wagon shop for George?

George thought of Jennie Gilfillan, too, as the slow miles rolled away behind his grating wagon wheels. He remembered the swish of her plaid skirt flying in the wind when she ran from him, and the waving curls that hung in clusters at the back of her head. He must try to do more than get her message to her father. If it was possible, he would learn something about the man and how he actually did work and live. If he had no home for her, and Ramsay had only the kitchen of the inn, hers was indeed a sorry state of affairs.

Then there was the National Pike to think about, and Mr. Wilkins' desire to know about it. It was near the end of a day of hazardous driving over a rutted, muddy, stone-filled road when George first heard the sound of voices in the distance—a roar of shouts and yells and occasional robust singing. He was anxious to see this famous Pike now that he was upon it, and his excitement mounted as the crescendo rose. Rounding a hill he came full upon the crew and he pulled his horses to a halt.

Stretching ahead was a strip about four rods wide which had been cleared of trees and underbrush, and down the center oxen and horses were straining at jangling chains to grub out roots and level a roadbed thirty feet wide. On either side there was a ditch for drainage. Behind the men with their animals were the pick and shovel workers, then men covering the surface with broken stone.

George had decided how he would go about trying to get information and he questioned the first group he came to. The men were sitting beside the road hammering at rocks, many with hands bandaged in dirty rags.

"Where's the contractor to be found?" George asked. "Mordecai Cochran's the name, isn't it?"

"Sure, an' what would ye be wantin' of that old devil?"

"I'm looking for a man named Gilfillan."

"Never heered the name but the superintendent's shack is up ahead."

Most of the men had stopped working to stare at George, glad for any opportunity to rest, it appeared.

"How's the road coming?" he asked.

"It's goin' as much as comin'," one man offered and the others laughed in bitter agreement. "Go back where we crossed over into Pennsylvany an' ye can't tell whether we bin there or not. Ask us? We don' know neither!"

"When will you get to Wheeling?"

"About 1850 an' may we live that long! What with everythin' breakin' down an' wearin' out, an nobody knowin' what they're about."

The grumbling was punctuated with unsavory descriptions of the contractor, the surveyors and every man in the capacity of boss.

"Fools! An' that's what we be, too. Twenty-five cents a day's what we git fer smashin' our fingers an' breakin' our backs."

George made his way past the laborers' camps where iron kettles hung over open fires, giving forth the strong scent of bear or deer stew. Pans of biscuits baked in the embers, and rows of pies stretched out on the ground nearby. Beyond were the forges where blacksmiths mended broken tools and shod horses, and finally there was a small shack, shoddily put together. George stood at the doorway, unnoticed at first. Here, too, there was arguing and grumbling.

"Seventy-five cents for sharpening a pick! Outrageous! We can't go on paying it," he heard a man say angrily.

"What are you going to do?" a second voice asked. "That's what the robber is charging. We pay it or he'll pull out, he says."

"Twenty-five cents for fixing a bucket hoop . . . a dollar and a half for putting iron tires on a wagon wheel. . . . Somebody'll have to go back and ask Congress for more money or we'll never get to Wheeling."

A man in buckskin trousers and jacket swung from the table where he had been looking at papers and hurled an empty tobacco can viciously out of the door. George jumped aside just in time to avoid a painful blow.

"What the . . . who are you?" the man demanded.

"I'm a wagoner—George Bauman," George said reaching for his hat to be sure it still was on his head. "Are either of you Mordecai Cochran?"

"No! What do you want?"

The tone didn't indicate that George would get it, whatever he wanted. If the tobacco can had hit him full in the face this ruffian doubtless would not have cared. George was sure he would get no cooperation, but he was forced to inquire for Gilfillan.

"We've no time to be looking over the laborers' rolls. You can wait for Cochran if you want to."

George gave a quick look at the rough bunks, tables, and benches in the shack. Gunter's scales and dividers, chains and compass littered the floor, and maps were tacked on all four walls. He was conscious that he, too, was being observed.

"So you're a wagoner," the second man said and his tone was not so unfriendly. "Which way are you going?"

"To Wheeling, and I'll be glad when the road gets through," George said. "When can we expect it finished?"

"At the rate we're going, about another year. You might find Cochran about a mile farther on. Look for a shack like this one."

George thanked him. He had gotten an honest answer to his question this time he was sure, and he was glad to be on his way. His horses would have had a good rest while he was at the road camp and now they would have to hurry along to catch up with the other drivers before nightfall.

George had no difficulty, a few days later, in finding the trader's post to which Ramsay had directed the wagoners. It was the first one he came to on the road leading into Wheeling. A high, weather-beaten board fence shut off the yard on three sides and within the compound was an unpainted store building and an inn for wagoners.

David McKeeb, proprietor of the post, was a busy, talkative man who had seen them coming while they were still a long way off and was waiting for them. He was dressed in the deerskin trousers and jacket which seemed to be the common garb of men in this frontier country.

"How's Fort Pitt?" he called out when George halted his horses in front of the trading post. He took off his hat, revealing heavy black hair like the growth of beard on his cheeks, and gestured toward the inn.

"Better put your horses up before the barn's full. There's snow in the air. You can unload tomorrow while they're resting."

The inn was no better and no worse than many George had seen in the days since he left Lancaster. From the big room where he would sleep on the floor again, he had a glimpse of the kitchen. It was little more than a smoke-filled hole with a floor of earth, but by this time George had almost forgotten his mother's scrubbed floor boards and shining kettles and neatly swept fireplace.

George had expected to inquire about Jennie's father from the innkeeper, but before he had a chance to talk to the man, McKeeb had joined the wagoners from Pittsburgh and was questioning them in a quick, eager voice.

How was the road? How many days had it taken them to get down from Fort Pitt? Where did they come upon the Pike? Finally, "How is my friend Ramsay?"

"He's fine," George told him. "Business seems to be good and Ramsay is doing well."

"I'm glad for Ramsay's sake," McKeeb said. "The National Pike'll result in the decline of Pittsburgh and I'd feared for his business."

From what little George had seen of Wheeling while he approached the town it scarcely seemed possible.

"When do you expect the Pike to be finished?" George asked.

"Within a year. Then you'll see all the traffic coming here, and it will pleasure me. But I can't help fearing for my friend even while I expect to profit myself."

The words were generous but there was something about the tone that made George distrust the man, and he hesitated to ask about Jennie's father.

"Is this the inn where most wagoners stop?" George asked. "If it is, the innkeeper is in a way to increase his business, too."

"This is the place," McKeeb assured him. "Old Ebenezer

Zane's tavern is farther on in town, but it's more for the gentry. Zane's been dead this five years but the place still carries his name and the road west into Ohio's still 'Zane's Trace.'"

"Is that the road the trappers follow?"

McKeeb nodded. "And the immigrants and wagoners. All coming through Wheeling now."

So this was the place where George must inquire about Robert Gilfillan, and likely McKeeb was the man. He might as well ask the question and see what answer he got.

"Perhaps you'd know about a man named Robert Gilfillan." George tried not to make the question seem important.

"H-m-m-m-m. . . . Gilfillan. . . . A trapper, you said?"

McKeeb wasn't looking at him. He was scratching his head and looking at the innkeeper.

"That's what I understand," George said.

"Gilfillan. . . . He isn't a friend of yours then?"

"I never saw him," George admitted. "If he stops here, I've a message to leave for him. I'll ask the innkeeper."

"So many stop here it's hard to remember all the names," McKeeb told him. "Then a lot are just known as 'Indian Joe' or something like that. Still, the name is familiar. I'll look on my books tomorrow. Remind me in the morning."

He sat for a time talking with the men and asked no further questions. George had thought he might inquire of the innkeeper after McKeeb left, but he observed that McKeeb timed his leave-taking to the very moment when the innkeeper went into the kitchen. Between those two there was close understanding, George was sure. It was even possible that McKeeb had an interest in the inn as well as the trading post. Perhaps he would do well to see what might be known at Zane's tavern before asking any further questions here.

Snow fell in the night and the air was crisp and cold the next morning. Unloading the heavy kegs of nails was a man-sized job and with good-natured rivalry the wagoners sought to surpass each other in speed and neatness, rolling the kegs to the place McKeeb designated. When he had finished, George set out to explore Wheeling and particularly to find Zane's tavern. With only a dozen stores in the town he experienced no difficulty. Zane's, however, was not the place where trappers stopped, or wagoners either, and the innkeeper had never heard of Robert Gilfillan.

A group of townsmen were finishing their noon meal when George asked his question and one motioned George to join him. He appeared to be a man of position for he was dressed in a suit of wool cloth and his hair and beard were neatly trimmed.

"I heard you inquire for Gilfillan," he said. "Is he a friend of yours?"

"No, but I had a message to leave, if I could find where he does business in Wheeling."

"I wish he did business with me," the man said. "I have a trading post and general store. Sometimes he comes to me for some small supplies but more often he goes to McKeeb's place on the outskirts. I understand he was in Wheeling with his furs just last week but I didn't see him, and now he won't be back until spring, likely."

The news did not surprise George too much, but it was disturbing. McKeeb could not be trusted to give Jennie's message to her father, he felt certain.

"Does Gilfillan have a home here? Or anywhere else?" George asked. "The message I have for him is from his daughter."

The merchant shook his head. "Gilfillan's probably one of the richest trappers who comes in from the Ohio country," he told George. "He lives like an Indian though, camping here and there and working with traps and gun all the time. He's not a man to talk much. I didn't know he had a family."

"Only one daughter, I think," George said. "The word she wanted to get to him is that Mrs. Ramsay is dead."

The merchant repeated the name. "I'll remember and tell him if I see him."

George tramped all over Wheeling before he went back to McKeeb's trading post. Mr. Wilkins probably would be interested in the size of the town and the indications of business. George found the levee almost deserted and no boats moving in or leaving, but the snow squalls would account for that. Zane's Trace, leading into Ohio, was a good road, however, and apparently well travelled. But there were no such factories here as George had seen in Pittsburgh and probably no more than one hundred houses. Wheeling was scarcely one-tenth the size of Pittsburgh. It would have a long way to go before it became the "Gateway to the West."

George had not made up his mind whether to mention Gilfillan again when he got back to the trading post. He was worried for Jennie. The little news he had for her was not reassuring. He walked slowly into the inn yard and to the barns to see to his horses, conscious uncomfortably that something was wrong.

His wagon! It wasn't where he had left it.

George rushed around the high wall to the trading post adjoining the inn, to find his white-topped vehicle drawn up to the back of the building. Two men were loading it with bags of grain from another wagon. This was a most unusual procedure. Wagoners loaded their own wagons.

"That's my wagon!" George shouted. "What's going on?"

"McKeeb's orders," they said and didn't turn to look at George. McKeeb came out at the sound of their voices.

"This grain came in while you were away and the farmers wanted to unload right away and be gone," he explained. "I saw no reason for handling it twice, so I had it put on your wagon. Less work for you."

"Where are the other drivers who come with me?" George asked, still suspicious of the move. None was in sight.

"Getting their loads. They said they'd like to start in the morning."

George was ready to start, too. He had no liking for this man, nor for the town either.

"By the way," McKeeb said, motioning George inside the store. "I looked up the records and find you're right. Gilfillan's a trapper and he brings his furs here. Was in town just this month, in fact."

Perhaps McKeeb had surmised George would get the information elsewhere. In any event, there was nothing to be gained by not giving him Jennie's message.

"What!" McKeeb exclaimed at the news. "My poor friend Ramsay. I haven't seen Mrs. Ramsay since...."

George wasn't listening. All he wanted was for morning to come, and to see the end of Wheeling. If McKeeb was a man to be trusted, then he was no judge of men.

CHAPTER

6

FURS FOR THE SEABOARD

George drove second in the wagon train which wound its slow way back to Pittsburgh. Behind him was the broad Ohio, wild ducks and geese riding the shallow shore waters; a wilderness of trees along its banks. Ahead was the rugged hill climb.

The wagons were keeping close together for the road was rough and the weather bad. Frequently the drivers had to stop to grease their wheels and rest their horses. George was acquainted with the men now. All were regulars who had made the trip before, and the owner of the three wagons was Christian Kline who drove first, as he had done on the trip to Wheeling.

Winter had wrapped the hills and forest knee deep in glistening whiteness. Christmas would come while George was making his way back to Pittsburgh—the first Christmas he had ever spent away from home. With a twinge he thought of Mem and Pep, his brothers and sisters. He could see Grossedawdi Eschleman disguised as the hideous "Belsnickle" who went looking for naughty boys and girls on Christmas Eve. Grossedawdi would put nuts and cakes on the floor to tempt Jacob and little Diederick. Barbara was too old now to be fooled. Why, Bevy would be fifteen! He had forgotten her birthday. He wondered if Diederick would touch the forbidden goodies the Belsnickle laid out. Even if he did, George knew Chris Kindle would come in the night and bring gifts for all the children. Somehow Mem always had gifts as well as Christmas cakes for everyone.

It would be just as well if he didn't think too much about Bevy and Jacob and Diederick. Perhaps the inn where they stopped on Christmas Eve would have a special dinner though, and the men might sing Christmas songs that night instead of "Barbara Allen" and "Darby Ram."

George's homesick thoughts were interrupted by the sudden, silent, animal leap of a man who had been concealed in the woods close to the road. Before he could realize what had happened, Barney had been jerked to a halt and George, astride the wheel horse, was looking straight into the barrel of a Lancaster rifle.

"Stay where ye are an' keep shet!"

The man spoke in a deep voice and his gun was pointed straight at George. His hat was low over his eyes and his coat high up around his nose. It was almost impossible to see his face. Only slits showed, where small, dark eyes glistened.

Another movement in the brush and a second man with two horses ran from the woods to the back of the wagon. Wasser rushed at him, growling menacingly. A yelp told George that the dog had been driven off with a vicious blow. He turned to see what was happening but the man in front spoke again.

"Jest keep lookin' ahead if ye want to live to find out what's goin' on behind."

George heard the grate of the end boards. He had caught only a glimpse of the second man. Buckskin clothing, heavy boots, head and face swathed in a scarf, hid any identifying features.

Wasser barked again and howled when he was hit once more. That his dog was being abused was worse for George to endure than the threat of the gun in front of him.

George tried to see the face of the man with the gun. Were these the two who had loaded his wagon the day before? He had not seen their faces, either. But how little grain they would be able to carry away on the backs of two horses! It seemed ridiculous that they would attempt to rob a six-ton load with no vehicle of their own. There must be a wagon somewhere in the woods or this robbery would not be worth the trouble.

George did not know whether the second man was armed. He thought of lashing suddenly with his Louden whip at Sall, shouting for help, and trying by the unexpectedness of the horses' lunge to dash the gun out of the man's hand. The villain was forcing the lead horse's head low to the ground and would not hesitate to shoot if he kept his hold on the gun, George was sure. Both he and the horse could be injured or killed. Would a few bags of grain warrant such a risk?

Beads of sweat stood out on George's forehead. From the corner of his eye he saw the second man tossing bags across the backs of his pack horses—bags which had been fastened together so they hung like a saddle. Who had tied them in that fashion? The men at McKeeb's post were the two, he was sure. They were the ones who were robbing him now, but it was difficult to understand their purpose. They could take so little.

For no reason at all George's mind went back to stories he had heard of the Whiskey Rebellion of a few years before. A pack horse could carry only four bushels of rye but it could carry the equivalent of twenty-four bushels when distilled into whiskey. He'd heard men talking of those troublesome days when Pennsylvania's distillers had threatened the very Union. Strange that it should come to his mind at a time like this. . . . Only that grain was being carried off on the backs of pack horses. . . .

Two shots, fired in rapid succession, interrupted his strange thinking. Before his astonished eyes the rifle that had been trained on him shot into the air and fell into the snow.

"George! Get that gun!"

It was the voice of Christian Kline!

George had no time to look for the wagoner. Off Bill's broad back . . . one foot on the whiffletree . . . a dash around the horses for the gun which now lay at Sall's feet.

A powerful kick in the shoulder and George was face down in the snow, clinging to the gun he had stooped to pick up. The man was upon him, and with grunts and curses they rolled in the snow at the feet of the animals. Then George heard another voice.

"Don't be a blasted fool! Get to the woods! There are teams ahead and behind."

The gun was slowly being pulled from George's grip but he fought to hold it. Unexpectedly the man who lay full upon him screamed in agony and his fingers loosened their hold. George raised his back and with a violent jerk tossed his assailant off into the snow. Blood was streaming from the man's face. For a second George could not understand what had happened. Christian Kline had not shot again and was not in sight.

Struggling to his feet, the gun still safely in his fists, George saw what had driven the robber off. Sall was shaking her head and spitting a hunk of felt from her bloodstained teeth.

Groaning and cursing, her victim dashed into the woods leaving his torn hat behind, and in seconds the two men and their pack horses were hidden by the trees.

George raised the rifle to his shoulder. He could shoot the man behind perhaps, but the other with the animals and bags of grain already was out of sight.

"Don't shoot," he heard Kline saying. "They didn't get enough. The other fellow can shoot too."

"Where were you?" George asked, lowering the gun. "How?" He was still gasping for breath. Wasser, limping and with a bloody neck, came whining to him for comfort.

"When your bells stopped ringing I thought something might be wrong. I was only a few rods ahead, but I had to keep out of sight. I had to climb into a tree where I could shoot the gun out of his hand without injuring the horses," Kline explained.

"I wonder about the driver behind," George asked. "I can't hear his harness bells, either."

"Something must have held him back," Kline said, looking to the trail behind. "Maybe an axle. . . . Maybe he saw them. . . ."

George stroked Sall's nose and pointed to the bloody hat lying in the snow.

"Sall got me a good Lancaster rifle," he said. "It must be worth almost as much as the grain they got. I can't understand. They had no wagon. At least none was in sight."

He looked toward the woods and the tracks in the snow. "It wouldn't be worth the risk to follow, would it?" he asked Kline. "They could ambush us."

"Could and would," Kline said, walking toward the back of the wagon. "Even though they know there are four armed men behind them now. How many bags did they get?"

"I'm not sure, but I don't think more than eight or ten

bags," George answered but as he spoke Kline's words began to puzzle him. "Four armed men, you said? You and the other drivers are armed? And you think the robbers know it?"

"All of us were armed but you," Kline told him. "Ramsay thought it wiser if you weren't, since you'd not carried firearms before. We'd be better able to protect you than you yourself, he thought."

Kline peered into the darkness of the loaded wagon, feeling of the bags. What had he meant? That Ramsay had anticipated this robbery?

The blood began pounding in George's temples. He stepped nearer to the rear of his wagon and looked observantly at the bags. He could see nothing suspicious about them.

"So Ramsay knew I was to be held at the point of a gun and robbed," George said slowly, his anger mounting. "There's more to this than I understand, Kline. And I don't like the sound of it."

Kline turned from his inspection of the wagon to face George. "If you'd known there would be furs hidden in your wagon, and that furs had been stolen before, would you have risked this haul?"

"Furs?"

"The third top of this load. He had you protected, afore and behind, with armed men."

George drew a long breath. Wasser was whimpering and he bent over to stroke the animal.

"A lot Ramsay cares about me or my dog," George muttered. "We might both have been killed. And the horses too."

"Not if you kept your head," Kline said. "He figured you to be cool-headed."

When George did not answer, Kline turned his attention to Wasser. The dog had an ugly gash in his neck.

"Put him up in the wagon where he can rest and lick himself," Kline suggested. He gave George a hand with the dog, closed the end boards, and looked down the road for the wagon behind, which still was silent.

"Getting the furs through is Ramsay's business, George," Kline said. "They're his furs. He bargained with Gilfillan to trap 'em and with McKeeb to ship 'em to Pittsburgh instead of Baltimore, but he's having trouble this winter."

"I still say I should have been told!"

Kline shrugged. "Perhaps. The wagoner whose load was robbed last time wouldn't make the trip again, nor will you if I guess right. He wasn't hurt no more'n you, but he lost half his load before the bells on the wagon behind warned the robbers off."

The bells on the wagon following George began ringing while Kline spoke and in a few minutes the third man in the team drew to a halt behind George and came running.

"The dirty swine pulled a log across the road just after you'd rounded the hill, George," he said between gasps. "I had to un-hitch and get my chain and haul it out of the way before I could go on. I didn't dare leave my horses alone."

George was still too angry to thank either of the men for their efforts on his behalf. They both had known he was in danger, but both had followed Ramsay's instructions and let him drive into it.

Kline, at least, recognized how George felt.

"Don't be too hard on Ramsay," he advised, starting ahead toward his own load, rifle in hand and eyes alert. "Every other load has got through and no trouble. He didn't know you'd be robbed and he hoped you wouldn't be. Don't worry about another attempt on this trip, either. It's right along here, near where the National Pike comes in, that they operate. They've got a trail through the woods to the new road, or I miss my guess. We could follow it now, in this snow, only it wouldn't be worth the risk as you said."

Both drivers left George to return to their own loads and for a moment he stood beside Sall, stroking her in silent gratitude. Except for the bite she had taken at the robber's face, he might have gotten as mean a beating as Wasser had suffered. He looked down at the rifle he had gained through the skirmish and wondered what to do with it. Riding Bill and holding it would be uncomfortable. He decided to store it on the load. If Kline was right, he'd have no further use for it.

George went over in his mind, again and again, what he would say to Ramsay when he reached Pittsburgh. For all of Kline's explanation, he felt tricked. Ramsay should have told him the whole truth.

And Jennie Gilfillan. Did she know about these robberies and, without actually doing so, still urge him to make the trip?

What about Mr. Wilkins? How much did he know about Ramsay and the fur business? He, at least, had warned George.

7

FINGER OF SUSPICION

The usual state of noisy confusion prevailed at Ramsay's inn when George and Kline arrived at last in Pittsburgh. From the forge came the clang of blacksmiths' hammers, drivers shouted to each other to give room, while harness bells chimed in various keys.

Because of the importance of the load he drove and the knowledge that Ramsay had anticipated trouble, George had expected the innkeeper to be on the lookout for him, but only the wagoners were in the yard with the stable boy. His deference to regulars and insolence to militia had not changed.

Nothing had changed. When at last the horses were watered, fed, and safe in the stable for the night, George went inside. Ramsay was at his usual perch, marking up "P's" for the drivers who bought pints, "Q's" for those who ordered quarts, and quietly refusing to sell more when he thought a man had drunk enough. The nod of greeting he gave George was the same silent recognition accorded all wagoners and he made no move to ask for a report.

Ramsay, George realized, ordinarily did not need to ask questions. The wagoners talked freely and in voices that would carry well beyond the walls of the inn.

"You, Bauman, how's the road to Wheeling?" one of the drivers asked.

"Rutted, and a hard, uphill haul back," was all George had to say. Indignant as he felt, the robbery was Ramsay's loss and he would not be the one to tell of it to anyone else. Not until he had finished his schnitz und knepp and coffee did he go to the bar where Ramsay held forth, and not until they were alone did he report.

"Your load is safe in the yard, Mr. Ramsay, with only eight or ten bags missing."

Ramsay scarcely turned his head. His watchful eyes moved slowly from one group of wagoners to another. Only the sudden set of his jaw acknowledged the news.

"How many attacked you?" he asked at last in a low voice.

"Two." George waited. Unless Ramsay wanted to ask questions—well, he could hold his tongue too.

"There's flour for Philadelphia and more nails for Wheeling," Ramsay said at last.

"I'll take the flour. My dog's in no condition to go to Wheeling again."

George did not try to keep the resentment out of his voice. The least Ramsay might have done was express some concern. Now he would ask one of the barmaids for a plate of food for Wasser and warm milk, if he could get it. Ramsay stopped him, however, when he turned away from the bar.

"There was a robbery in the Harrisburg hills last week too, Bauman," the innkeeper said. "I didn't know that you would be attacked. I had no knowledge." Then, his voice changing,

"Now tell me about your dog. We've got a supply of medicines here."

For the first time George and Ramsay looked each other full in the face. The eyes of the old Scott were knowing—shrewd, perhaps—but the look was level and honest. "Tell me about your dog," he repeated.

So George told the whole story and Ramsay listened without interrupting.

"Your Sall's teeth will have left a scar," he said when George had finished and he nodded as though well satisfied. "Come and I'll see that Wasser is well cared for."

It was a surprise when Ramsay motioned him inside the kitchen and at once George looked for Jennie. She was at the far end of the room, standing on a small box to put dishes into a cupboard too high for her to reach the shelves. Ramsay called to her at once: "Jennie Gilfillan!"

Her eyes were anxious when she swung around. At the sight of George she half smiled, then looked at the innkeeper waiting his orders.

"Is there any salve here, and liniment, or is it all at the stable?" Ramsay asked. "Bauman's dog has a gash in its neck. I guess it hasn't been fed yet either."

The door closed behind him and Jennie ran quickly to George, her eyes eager and her smile disarming.

"George! Your poor dog!" She turned to the older woman. "Mary, where is the liniment? I'll warm milk, and there's lots of food."

Mary, who had seemed to be standing guard over the girl when George last saw her, now stared in open-mouthed surprise, hands on her hips. With a stolid, "Well, I never!" she got the medicine while Jennie put milk to warm on the front of the big iron stove and filled a plate with food. Mary offered no protest when Jennie whipped her coat from a nail near the door and with food and medicine, followed George into the yard of the inn.

"George, tell me," she said as soon as they were alone. "Did you learn anything?"

"Not much. Come this way."

She seemed to understand at once that he had no good news to tell her. "What happened to your dog?" she asked, the eagerness gone from her voice.

George was not certain how much he should tell. Now that he saw Jennie again he was sure she had not known of the danger in his trip to Ohio.

"What happened?" she repeated.

"We met some villains on the way back," George said evasively. "Wasser rushed out barking and got beaten for his pains. He has a stiff leg and a wound on his shoulder that's still raw."

"This will fix it," Jennie promised. "Mr. Ramsay has good medicines. He learned about them when he was a boy in Scotland. I'm glad nothing happened to you, George."

He helped her climb up into the wagon and called softly to Wasser who crawled over the bags to come to them. Under the wagon top it was not cold and the bags were soft to sit upon.

"No, nothing happened to me," George repeated. "Why did you say that?"

"Because once early this winter a wagoner lost a whole load of furs he was bringing to Mr. Ramsay," Jennie answered without hesitation. "He fought them, and was beaten, and when he got here it was a bad night at the inn. He was going to beat Mr. Ramsay, but some of the other wagoners held him off. It was really terrible."

"You saw it? You weren't in the big room too?"

"We couldn't have missed knowing about that, Mary and I," Jennie told him. "What with the men shouting and fighting each other and tables and chairs knocked over. The barmaids all came running to the kitchen."

Inwardly George sighed with relief. Jennie knew nothing of the subsequent robberies nor of the arrangement Ramsay had made with Kline to protect his furs on the trip George had just completed. He was ashamed he had ever mistrusted her.

"Is Mary good to you?" he asked.

"Oh, yes. She used to work in the kitchen for Mrs. Ramsay. Now she works in the kitchen here. If it wasn't for her, I don't know what I'd do. You . . . you didn't get any news at all?"

It was hard to tell her, but she must be warned not to go to Ohio unless her father knew she was coming and made some plan for her. She took the news in silence. One gentle hand stroked Wasser and George wondered if, in the darkness, she was crying.

"Jennie, why is it you want to leave Mr. Ramsay?" George asked. "You haven't told me all, I'm sure."

He heard her catch her breath and she did not answer at once.

"Don't you want to tell me?"

"What's to become of me, George?" she finally asked. "I work all day with Mary in the kitchen. Hard work. At night we crawl up into one little room above, to sleep. The girls and boys I knew at school never come here, to the wagoners' inn, and I can't get away. He pays Mary, but to me he gives no money. And each day I see him getting more closed up like. Less and less he thinks of either of us. At first Mary said he would get married again and open up the big house, and we'd go back. Now she says all he thinks of is the money he makes, though what he's to do with it we don't know."

"Your father has money too," George told her. "They say he's one of the richest fur traders who come to Wheeling."

"Money!" Her voice trembled. "What help is it to me? And what am I to do? Has my father . . . forgotten me?"

"He couldn't forget you, Jennie," George declared. "How could he? He thinks you're well cared for with Mrs. Ramsay. But I left word in two places in Wheeling. If either message gets to him he'll come for you I'm sure."

"You . . . you heard nothing . . . bad? You're telling me all?"

"Of course, Jennie. Why?"

When she answered her voice was scarcely a whisper. "Mr. Ramsay suspects my father. Only he and Mr. McKeeb could have known when the furs left Wheeling and what wagon carried them."

The words shocked George into silence. Only McKeeb and the men who had loaded his wagon knew which team to stop and which wagon to rob on this last trip too. One of the two thieves would carry incriminating scars the rest of his life. How could George know Robert Gilfillan was not the man, or his companion?

"So you see, George," he heard Jennie saying, "I've got to get word to my father. I can't stay here at Mr. Ramsay's sufferance when he thinks such a thing."

"But you can't go now, Jennie!" His hand touched her arm as though to hold her back. "You can't go to Ohio alone. McKeeb's inn in Wheeling . . . it's so much worse than this, you can't imagine."

"But I'm proud too!"

What was he to say? "If either of my messages gets through, he'll come," George heard himself saying but in his heart he felt little assurance. "If he doesn't, by the time I come next winter, I'll go to Wheeling again, I promise."

"Next winter!" It was almost a sob. In the darkness she fumbled for the flap of the wagon and with a choked "good night" she left him.

It was hard for George to sleep that night, what for re-living the robbery and thinking of Jennie Gilfillan. She was on his mind the next day, too, when he made his way to the bank to report what he had learned of the National Pike to Mr. Wilkins. Had he any knowledge of the men or of affairs in Wheeling, or of the robberies?

George had not felt uncomfortable with Mr. Wilkins either at the Old Sorrel tavern or during their long walk about Pittsburgh, but inside the austere banking house with its cages of heavy wire and massive furniture he was not at home. He was conscious of his homespun clothing and heavy boots while he waited until at last a clerk took him to the banker's office.

"George Bauman! Sit down and let's hear about Wheeling. Have a cigar. What? Conestoga wagoner who doesn't smoke a 'stogie?' Neither do I. It's a filthy habit. Well, what about Wheeling?"

"It's not one-tenth the size of Pittsburgh and it hasn't the coal or iron," George reported. "No industry to speak of. But the road will be through next year and the town is expecting a big business boom because of the emigrants."

"Emigrants alone won't make Wheeling a great city," Mr. Wilkins said positively. "Remember those you saw on our levee last month? Look again in the spring before you leave on your last trip. You'll see them camped along the roads leading into Pittsburgh. They don't buy much here and they won't in Wheeling, either. After they get settled and have raised a crop or two, they'll have money to buy the things they need. And Pittsburgh's going to keep on making them."

"Like nails?" George asked.

"And tools and window glass and hardware. Wagons too. We should build wagons."

"Aren't any wagons built here now?" George asked.

Mr. Wilkins shook his head. "There are four or five who call themselves wagonmakers, but they don't build like yours and they haven't a factory like I've shown you. What farmers in the flat Ohio and Kentucky land need is a lighter but well built wagon, for hauling grain and produce. I've been there and I know what they need. I have a brother in Kentucky. My grandfather trapped in Ohio."

George had seen a few lighter wagons on the road near Pittsburgh but he thought little of them. They would carry no great loads of iron ore or limestone or hogsheads of molasses, but it was true the farmers and trappers had no such loads to transport.

"Wheeling probably has an advantage in the river," George suggested. "It's wider and more navigable, I was told."

"Water travel still is more hazardous," Mr. Wilkins replied. "Currents and snags and falls. And travelers can't band themselves together for protection so well as wagon teams."

Once more George wondered what Mr. Wilkins knew of the need for protection and whether he should mention the robbery, but Mr. Wilkins went on talking.

"Our state took the lead in road building when we started the old Philadelphia-Lancaster Pike, and we'll see that we keep ahead. Without any Congressional politics too. We'll build our own roads with our own private capital backed by our own state government. And we'll keep ahead of Wheeling!"

Mr. Wilkins was very serious. He got up and looked out into the rutted, muddy street and a wry smile twisted his lips.

"We've got some work to do yet, I'll admit, and I haven't convinced the Common Council of it yet, either."

George rose too, and offered his hand in parting.

"Look me up whenever you come to town," Mr. Wilkins said. "If you ever decide to leave Lancaster County let me know. You might. My family did."

His smiling eyes and gracious manner held an invitation. It was good to know this man. George had never thought of leaving Lancaster County until Johannes had said one of them must go. The thought had been in the back of his mind, like a half-believed ghost story, ever since. It brought back the picture of home again, now while George walked slowly to the inn. Pep and Grossedawdi Eschleman would soon start preparing the land for the garden and crops. On Gertrude's Day, March 17, the cabbage must be planted. He had to be home by the time the moon was waxing in the month of March, for seed planted in a waxing moon grew more rapidly than if planted when the moon was waning. When the horns of the moon were down the onions would be planted, and St. Benedict's, March 21, was the day to secure a good onion crop. Beans and early potatoes were always planted when the horns of the moon were up. It was important that the ground be ready when the moon was right.

Then would come the months for growing and ripening when he would work in the wagon shop, and finally harvest and November, when he would go hauling again. He would drive his own new wagon down to Wheeling and over Zane's Trace into Ohio if need be, next winter. He had promised.

But it was an eternity of time away.

8

BLUE HILLS OF HOME

When George came to the wooden covered bridge over the Conestoga Creek, he was home. There were still a few miles to go, but here were Chestnut Ridge and Turkey Hill and the Welsh Mountains rising six hundred feet or more above the creek land. Up at Elizabeth Furnace by a pass in South Mountain, Baron Von Stiegel had started his glass manufacturing plant fifty years ago. It all came back to George while he hurried the horses along.

Last night the great horned owl tore the darkness with demonic screams and the thunderous croaking of frogs until the late hours prophesied plentiful rains and prosperous crops. Wasser had sniffed the air with new enthusiasm this morning and seemed to understand when George had spoken to him.

"You get behind and push! We'll be home this afternoon."

George came to the blacksmith shop first. At the sound of

his rumbling, clattering wheels Gid Hefs left the forge and came racing toward him.

"George! It's about time. Johannes has been back a week already."

Gid's curling black hair was a damp, tangled mass and his bright eyes shone with welcome. He ran alongside the wheel horse George rode, slapping at the animal's flanks.

"Your horses look good. So do you. They must have fed you well at the inns."

"Good enough, but the kitchen at home is going to be a welcome sight. How have you been, Gid?"

"Busy. Wait until you see. I have all the iron work done for both our wagons."

"Both? When did you get the time?" George asked.

"There's not so much work at the forge in the winter," Gid reminded him. "Don't you remember last winter when we started the fish head pattern for me and the tulips for you?"

George remembered. There had been days when Shtuffle Henning, the big, slow-moving blacksmith, had allowed Gid to spend the entire time working at the decorative iron for the tool boxes, the hinges, the houndsbands and the ornate ironing for the end of tongue and doubletrees.

"You wouldn't waste a minute would you, old bag of energy!" George laughed and kicked good-naturedly at Gid's broad shoulders. Gid was well built, and the muscles of his arms and back were made for the heavy work in the forge. His hips were narrow and his legs long and slender. There was nothing fat or stocky about the blacksmith's apprentice.

"More fool I, if I did waste time," Gid replied. "I'm through this fall. And we've got wagons to build this summer. You know what your father promised if you and Johannes had a good winter, and Johannes said you did."

Well George remembered. He was to have a wagon of his own when he was eighteen, the same as Johannes. In return for the iron work Gid had done, Pep had promised him a wagon too, if he and George would help build it. Then Gid might spend next winter hauling, making use of the Bauman's young horses, while deciding where to locate as a blacksmith.

Three years ago the huge logs for the wagons had been cut into planks at the sawmill. Several log butts had produced the spokes and all had been split and hewn out of the rough by Pep's hand axe while George learned the skill. Then the wood had been ranked, with planks, spokes and hub boards in their proper places, and re-ranked twice. Now the swamp-grown wood, tough as whale bone, was aged and ready.

"We'll start on the wagons as soon as spring planting is done," George promised. "I can't wait to see the iron work."

"Come by the forge tonight after you've seen your folks," Gid invited. "I've so much to tell you. . . . You . . ." he hesitated and looked away. "But you must see your folks first."

"Now what have you been up to?" George laughed. "Always something."

"Tonight will be time enough to talk," Gid answered.

Pep, in the wagon shop near the house, was the first to see George. He shouted a welcome and at the sound of his voice Wasser rushed ahead to jump on him, almost knocking him over, although Pep was a big man weighing two hundred pounds. His hair was more gray than George remembered it and the lines around his eyes and from his nose to his rounding cheeks were deep, but for all that Pep did not look any older than many of the wagoners.

"Am I glad to see you!" George called, jumping from Bill's back and hurrying across the grass to his father's outstretched hands. It was indeed good to feel the friendly slap on his shoulders and then to see Mem running from the house, followed by the children.

"George! Yes, and you're a grown man now! Come to your old Mother!"

She was laughing and crying at the same time and hugging him close, while Jacob and Bevy and little Diederick all pulled at his legs and clamored for attention.

"Inside I have chicken corn soup and pot pie and schnitz . . ."

"He puts the horses up first, Mem," Pep interjected. "Then he can eat himself full."

George left the wagon at Pep's shop, boosted his sister and brothers onto the bays' broad backs, and with Pep walking beside him he merrily led the way down the road to Grossedawdi Eschleman's where the animals were kept. What a joy it was to be telling Pep about his trip, to see the valley greening and buds ready to burst on the Lombardy poplars that lined the road to the farm.

Grossedawdi was out on the land with Johannes, burning dry brush along the edges of the fields, but he had been expecting George and he came to the barns when he saw the Baumans arriving.

"Come inside for a piece of schnitz pie, Hon Yorick," Grossememmi called from the kitchen door and she gave his cheek a quick peck and squeezed his arm. She spoke in the German of the valley and the sound of her words alone was welcome enough for George.

"Mem has schnitz pie waiting at home," Bevy warned him, adding, "I made it myself."

"You are a big girl, aren't you?" George smiled. "Fifteen! I know." He pulled her taffy braids happily.

But Grossememmi was not to be done out of feeding him first, and George and Pep could do justice to two pieces of pie any day. How tasty it was, made with brown sugar and cream.

From Grossememmi's kitchen, where glasses of milk and wedges of pie were soon on the scrubbed-clean saw-horse table, George looked out at the big barn, built on the side of a hill to give it two levels. A ramp of stone led to the floor above where hay and wheat and oats were always stored for seed, with an area down the center kept clear for threshing out the grain. The ground floor was a warm home for horses, cows and calves, and storage space for Grossedawdi's wagons and farm tools. Chickens hid their nests in the stalls and mows, and many a lazy afternoon George had spent looking for eggs or idly day dreaming in that big barn.

George had thought Johannes would come in while they were eating, but it was not until all were home again and Mem and Bevy were setting places at the opened drop-leaf table in the Bauman kitchen that George saw his half-brother.

"So you're home at last," Johannes said cheerfully enough when he came into the room. "It's about time, for this is an early spring. The peach trees have already bloomed. Grand-pop and I were beginning to think you'd keep on wagoning until we had the crops all in."

Fruit trees blooming out of season was not a good sign, but Johannes refused to give credence to signs, and George ignored it now.

"Except we have my own wagon to make this summer, and Gid's too, I'd have liked well enough to make another trip down to Wheeling," George told him remembering Jennie Gilfillan. Jennie's story was the only thing he had not told Pep while they walked to the farm and back that afternoon.

"Pep, how many wagons must we build this summer?" George went on. "Will there be time I can spend on my own?"

"You'll have time. I seem to have built wagons for all in the valley already. The only work I have for the wheelrights now is repairs, and some lower wheels to make for wagons that will be used on the farm this summer, now that work on the road is over for the season."

"In Pittsburgh, the factory workers are all engaged in one place, not making separate parts of things in their own barns or shops, like here," George told his father. "We should set up our wagon shop like a regular factory."

"George, and you've a head full of ideas," Pep laughed. "Now Johannes was glad enough to get home and back to things as they are. But you!"

"Farming's no different anywhere," George commented. "It's the industry that's different."

"Even farming in Ohio?" Johannes asked taking his place at the table where the steaming pot pie beckoned, and taking care not to look directly at George or indicate too much interest.

"They use smaller and lighter wagons, but that's all I heard of that's different from here in the valley."

George knew Johannes was eager for news of Wheeling and the National Pike although he asked no more questions. It was Pep whose eyes were on George when he told of Zane's Trace leading through the new country and across Ohio.

A pounding on the kitchen door, and excited girls' voices interrupted the stories of the winter's experiences. Immediately George recognized Anna Showalter and Elizabeth Yoder as the ones who were calling Pep's name and his and Johannes'.

"Mr. Bauman!"

"Johannes!"

"George! Quick, there's a fire!"

The three bounded from the table to open the door upon

the frightened girls. Breathlessly, both trying to talk at once, they pointed to the roadway.

"Look! It's gaining. It's almost at your shop!"

Leaping, snake-like fingers of red, blue-black smoke billowing above, crept along the edge of the road through dead winter grass and leaves. In an instant the danger shot like the flames themselves through George's mind. Pep's wagon shop . . . the lumber for his own wagon and Gid's, lay in the path of the flames.

"Johannes! To Grossedawdi's for barrels of water! The horses are all there!" Pep ordered.

"He's coming already," Elizabeth told them. "We were there, visiting with Grossememmi Eschleman, when we saw it." She gasped for breath. "He put the barrels on the wagon and was harnessing the horses. He told us to run ahead and warn you."

Elizabeth's long face was never really pretty, but the fright and seriousness of the occasion gave it strength and intensity. Anna, after one terrified glance back at the roadway, started to run from the house.

"I'll go for Gid," she called back to them. "I'll tell my brothers." Then she was gone, her yellow curls flying behind her.

"There's an old wagon top in the shed," Pep said running from the house. "We'll wet it down . . . until Grossedawdi gets here. . . ."

They tore the heavy material into three strips, soaked it at the well, and raced to the fire. Their house was of stone and would not burn, but the wagon shop was of logs. Often Pep had talked of building a stone shop, it came back to George while he pounded at the flames. Other men had come, some with shovels to turn up fresh earth and stop the spreading blaze. It crackled and slithered through the dry brush and when they beat it back at one point it forged ahead in a new path, nearer Pep's sheds and the lumber for the two precious wagons.

Men were shouting, and women too, who had come to help smother the demon that now was creeping forward in the night. They had to control it! Grossedawdi's heavy wagon rattled along the roadway at last, bringing barrels of water which best of all would wipe out the flames.

Without looking up George knew that Gid was fighting beside him, his strong arms flailing wet bags against the surging menace. Another wagon came with more barrels of water . . . the Showalter boys. They were only fourteen and fifteen but they could help.

"Wet the grass in front of our lumber," Gid shouted. "Come, George! We've got to stop it! We've got to!"

They rolled the barrels down from the big red and blue Showalter wagon and soaked the grass all along the side of the shed, then with spades they dug up the earth. As George worked he felt an inward fury rising. Had Johannes deliberately been careless about the fire? Had he wanted it to flare up again and spread from the clearing beside the fields to the lumber which would give George and Gid wagons as good as his own? With wagons they would be as independent to leave the valley as he.

It was absurd. It was unreasonable. George told himself the wagons alone were not enough for any of them. Without horses none was free to go, and the horses belonged to Pep and Grossedawdi.

Yet with wagons, and the use of Pep's animals, they could work and earn money. . . . And Johannes' own wagon was safe from danger back at the farm, he recalled.

The thought was maddening and he could not drive it from his mind. With it came the remembrance of the cleft in the road . . . then the trip to Wheeling. Johannes had been ready enough for George to make that dangerous journey. Everyone had known of the danger. Johannes had sought no load to take to Ohio himself. . . .

They beat back the fire to a smouldering mass of fading smoke, and while the men watched it, and trampled on the last of the embers, George found his brother in the darkness.

"You! Johannes! You wanted this fire to eat up the lumber for my wagon!"

"What? Why, you . . . !"

Johannes wheeled on him and George swung without thinking. Before his angry eyes the steep hill rose again . . . the wagon tongue was ready to plunge into the upgrade again. . . . Sall's rearing lunge. . . .

He swung at Johannes with all the strength and fury that had forced the robber off his back into the snow beside the mountain trail to Wheeling. One solid blow! Another, and Johannes reeled backward in the darkness. Reeled and fell and was on his knees in an instant, but George pounced upon him like an animal.

A strong hand clamped over George's arm and he was jerked back, swung around, and set on his heels in the dirt.

"What's the meaning of this!" It was Pep. "Get up, both of you! I ask you a question."

George was not hurt and he was on his feet first.

"Johannes let this fire start deliberately," he charged. "He wanted to destroy the lumber for our wagons."

"George Bauman! With what reason do you say such a thing? Against your own brother!"

"I have reasons. He would have wrecked my wagon on the trip to Pittsburgh. He let me drive into danger, knowing of it He cared nothing for what calamity befell me."

Johannes was up now, denying it.

"That's not true! Until you went to Wheeling I was never far from you!"

"You warned me of the steep hill I couldn't make without unhitching, didn't you?" George demanded. "And the Indian bridges that weren't safe to cross. . . ."

"Who warned me of them?" Johannes asked. "Why should I coddle you?"

That was something George had not thought about. How had Johannes managed, that first winter when he tried his strength and judgment against the road?

"You were so ready to be a wagoner," Johannes shot the words at him. "You were so sure of yourself! You could manage horses and load without asking any questions of one who had been over the road before you. You were so strong! Did you ask anything of me?"

There was no answering those accusing words. George knew he had given no thought to the dangers when he started. He had, indeed, been sure he could manage team and load. He had been fearless. Not once had he asked Johannes' advice, it was true. Yet he tried to justify himself now.

"You were just waiting to claim my bells!" he charged. "You knew it would be a miracle if I got through that stark ravine."

"I got through and nobody warned me," Johannes said proudly. "Nobody took my bells!"

The men had gathered around them—Gid and the Showalter boys, Grossedawdie, Shtuffle Henning and the others. In the darkness George felt his cheeks begin to burn. Johannes was turning the tables on him, and suddenly he felt mean and ashamed of himself.

"As for this fire tonight, why should I want to burn your lumber?" Johannes demanded. "Why should I not want you to have a wagon—to go with, and stay gone!"

"Johannes!"

It was Pep again.

"I'm ashamed of both of you. Must you forever act like little boys, fighting in the schoolyard? You, George, to accuse your brother unjustly. And of such an unrighteous thing. You, Johannes! To say you would have your brother gone! To have such thoughts!"

They were silent before his rebuke, and the rightness of his judgment. Shamed at the note of sorrow in his voice.

"We will go now," Pep said firmly. "What must the neighbors think of us."

9

GHOST OF ROCK HOLLOW

George knew what was coming. He and Johannes followed Pep in silence into the big kitchen. Mem, the children, even Wasser seemed to know. Without a backward glance Bevy, Jacob and Diederick followed Mem upstairs to bed and Wasser curled himself beside the fireplace, burying his nose and eyes under a shaggy paw.

The Good Book lay beneath the almanac on the mantle and Pep took it down solemnly. He drew the lighted candles on the kitchen table nearer and opened the Bible deliberately. Deliberately, also, he chose the chapter he would read.

"Though I speak with the tongue of men and of angels and
      have not charity
   I am become as sounding brass, or a tinkling cymbal."

George knew the chapter but he listened. He knew what he

must do. When the reading ended he must tell Johannes he was sorry, for he was the one who had been in the wrong.

". . . Charity suffereth long and is kind; charity envieth not; charity vaunteth not itself, is not puffed up . . ."

Johannes must forgive, too, or the reading would go on. Pep would not necessarily stop with one chapter. His deep voice intoned the words slowly.

George's eyes strayed from his father's large frame and sober face to the familiar objects in the kitchen. Pewter plates and brown earthenware shone in the corner cupboard. Gay bunches of red peppers and ears of corn hung from the ceiling above; chairs and chests, bright with bird and flower designs in red and yellow, black and green, reflected in the mirror that hung above the shipping wheel. And the white wax candles and the stone pitcher for cider on the mantle—he had almost forgotten how bright and good-smelling Mem's kitchen was. If only the kitchen at Ramsay's inn was like this one—a place where the young people would come and visit Jennie. . . .

But the chapter was ending. This was not the time to think of Jennie.

"I was in the wrong," George admitted quietly. "I'm sorry, Johannes."

Johannes had been staring into the fireplace. He did not look up but he answered as was expected of him. "It's all right. I hold no grudge."

For a few moments Pep sat with his head in his hands. Perhaps he was praying. His children never knew, but until he dismissed them they were not free to go. At last he got up and put the Book away and he and Johannes went upstairs.

Before the fireplace Mem had put out the big wooden tub and soap and towels. Over the smouldering logs the huge iron kettles were filled with water, warming for George's bath. He needed it, and he scrubbed his body clean, wishing his mind could be wiped clean as easily. Johannes had said he forgave and that he held no grudge, but George wondered if his brother had really forgiven him.

More than ever he had cause to doubt it the following day. It was Sunday and all in the neighborhood gathered for services at the red brick church with its white trim. Families sat together and the Baumans, in one of the center pews, could both see and be seen. Once again George read the mottoes on the wall near the pulpit. They were written in the broken fractur lettering used on birth certificates and familiar sayings for hanging on parlor walls. "Liebe Gott Ueber Alles" and "Liebe deinen Naechsten." If he must love his neighbor, how much more he should love his brother, but it seemed to him Johannes made it very hard to do.

There had been little visiting in the churchyard before services, but afterward people clustered about, gathering leaves from the sides of the red sandstone grave markers, and visited.

"Mrs. Bauman, and your boys are both back now! How good, ya?"

"Did you get the onions all in, yet?"

"I have a new recipe. . . ."

George had heard the rooster, standing right in front of the kitchen door, crow loudly that morning. The gray and white pussy cat had licked himself clean and lay down in the sun, tail pointing toward the Yoder house. Sure signs, these, that company was coming. It was no surprise to hear Mem saying the Showalter young people and Elizabeth Yoder were to have Sunday dinner with them. It was a surprise, though, not to find Johannes in the churchyard when they were ready to go home.

"Johannes said not to wait for him," Bevy explained, a note

of importance in her voice, when Mem began hustling all to-gether. "Johannes said he was going for a walk and might not be home until night." Bevy was proud to have shared Johannes' confidence, George could see.

"A walk?"

Mem and Pep avoided looking at each other it seemed, and began almost too cheerfully to hurry the young people into the wagon. Nothing more was said about Johannes.

Anna and the Showalter boys were not disturbed and began singing hymns. Elizabeth, who couldn't carry a tune, tried to chime in but George was sure the day now was a disappoint-ment for her, and if Johannes did not come back the evening would be worse. Where had Johannes gone?

George wished his mother had invited Gid, too, but the blacksmith and his wife and Gid with them had left the churchyard together early.

"Hoongerich?" Mem asked when they piled out of the wagon and made for the cool shade beside the big stone house. "Soon you can eat yourselves full."

Mem's Sunday dinners were something to wait a week to get. Rivvel soup, boova shenkel with plenty of big chunks of beef, fresh peas made with butter balls, the sweets-and-sours, sticky cinnamon buns Bevy had made that morning. Then the pies. Rhubarb, cherry crumb, and schnitz of course, not to mention the gold cakes and raisin cakes and apple cakes. Over the noise of the dishes and the "Oh's" and "Ah's" as the food appeared, George forgot both Johannes and Gid.

They all saw Gid that afternoon, however.

"How do you like the iron work for your wagon?" Anna had asked George when at last they left the dinner table. Her round, blue eyes looked at him eagerly as though she wanted him to like it, then she looked away quickly.

"I haven't seen it yet," George had to admit. He hadn't seen it because of the unpleasant events of the night before and there was a moment of uncomfortable silence. "Maybe we could all go to the blacksmith shop now," he suggested. "More than likely Gid will be there."

Mem told them to run along. She had nothing to do but wash the dishes and get a few things ready for supper.

The blacksmith shop was a long, low, one-story stone building with wide doors at front and back. The forge was gray and dead today for no work was allowed by Shtuffle Henning on Sunday. Through the open doors George saw again the horseshoes hanging from giant nails in the walls, and the hooks, saws, and piles of coal that tomorrow would glow red in the forge from daylight until dark. Shtuffle was a tireless worker.

Gid was there alone, moving his iron work carefully. He had laid it out in the sunshine as though he expected them, and the ornate tulip pattern for George, the fish heads for himself, were beautiful. His face lightened when he saw the three Showalters and George and Bevy and Elizabeth, all eager to praise his workmanship. Clean and proper looking in his Sunday clothes, Gid was more handsome today than George had remembered him.

Anna at once bent over the hammer hasp and looked up at George. There the blacksmith always stamped his initials and the date, and on the work Gid had completed there was a strong "G. H. 1817."

"So you're a real blacksmith and no apprentice already?" George inquired. "That's fine." He wasn't too much surprised. Shtuffle had always favored Gid.

"Shtuffle Henning told him he could," Anna spoke up when Gid hesitated. She, too, seemed very proud of him.

"Only six more months," Gid reminded them. He didn't look at Anna or the Showalter boys but eyed his iron critically.

"When my apprenticeship is over you all know I get my own set of tools. . . ."

George knew. "And a sum of money and a whole suit of clothes," he finished. "It won't be long, Gid. There are things I want to tell you about Pittsburgh soon, and what I saw there."

There was a clamoring for George to tell of his adventures, and he was pleased to talk when they all sat down under the shade trees with Gid. No one mentioned the trouble of the night before or said anything about Johannes, but when the afternoon ended the Showalters invited Gid home with them instead of George, and George found himself taking Elizabeth back to the Bauman's for supper. This wasn't the way he would have planned it, and things were even more uncomfortable when he found Johannes had not come home when he and Bevy and Elizabeth got there.

"You must take Elizabeth home, George," his mother whispered to him when they left the supper table.

"What?" She nodded emphatically in answer.

George hadn't thought of taking Elizabeth home. He had never taken any girl home except Anna. He hadn't taken Anna home since the schnitzing party last fall. That, he recalled, had been fun with Anna running down the road and he after her, until at last they had walked quietly into her own yard, hand in hand in the moonlight.

This was different. Elizabeth, who had been quiet and polite all day, found her tongue in the fading light of evening while they walked along the road to the big Yoder house.

"Things are certainly getting different, aren't they?" she asked, laughing nervously. "I guess they do when we grow up."

"What do you mean?" George asked. What was she driving at? He glanced at the tall, somewhat angular figure beside him, her hair combed back in a proper, grown-up way. "How different?"

"Oh . . . Anna . . . Gid . . . you. . . ." Finally she said, slowly, "Johannes."

"I don't see what you mean," George repeated. "Just because Johannes went for a walk today—although I admit I don't know where he could have gone."

"I know," Elizabeth told him. "To Lancaster."

"How do you know?"

"My father saw him there one night last week. He went for a walk then, too. He was glad enough for a ride home, or he'd have been until morning."

"Lancaster," George repeated. "What did he go to Lancaster for?"

"He didn't tell, of course, but I could guess."

George thought he knew what Elizabeth's guess would be. Another girl. Elizabeth was old enough to be getting married and no boys in the neighborhood had paid much attention to her, for they were afraid of her father. Except that George was younger than she, he would have been afraid to take her home too. He was uncomfortable about it anyway, now that he thought about it, and they walked in silence listening to the croaking frogs and the night calls of the birds. Spring had really come early to the valley and the gold-green tassels of the oaks along the road swayed in the night breeze ahead of them.

Suddenly Elizabeth stopped, rigid, and the next instant the weird cry of a great horned owl echoed through the valley.

"I saw it!" she gasped and her hands tugged at George's coat and held to it with a locked grip.

"Sure, I saw it too," George said. "You've seen owls before, Elizabeth."

"It wasn't an owl. . . . I saw a white trail. . . . It was . . . the ghost from the rock hollow house!"

"Elizabeth! There are no ghosts."

The owl screeched again and ahead of them a cotton-tail rabbit raced across the road into an arbutus bank. Elizabeth clung to him tighter. In spite of himself George felt a chill along his spine and down his legs. Ghost stories he had heard since childhood. This was all nonsense. He knew it was nonsense but it was eerie just the same.

"Come on, Elizabeth. You know there are no ghosts."

Her teeth were chattering and she trembled as she pressed close to his side. "The rock hollow house . . ."

"The rock hollow house ghost disappeared right after old Betsy went down into the cellar with him and got all the money," George heard himself almost whispering the legend. "After he showed Old Betsy where he'd hidden the stolen money he was never seen again."

The night was suddenly very still, the owl out of sight. But Elizabeth did not loosen her hold on the collar of his coat.

"There was a long white trail after the owl flew . . . I saw it . . . following the owl."

"It was the tassels of the tree . . . or maybe buttermilk clouds."

George realized he was still whispering. Another bird cry and the branches ahead of them rustled strangely. George had to do something. They couldn't stand there all night listening to these uncanny noises and the hooting of the owl.

"Old Betsy buried that ghost a hundred years ago," George insisted. "We're going right under that tree and home to your house," he announced as boldly as he could. "Give me your hand now, Elizabeth."

He had to force her hands loose and take her firmly by one

arm. She was shaking as though she actually believed she had seen a ghost and George wondered if he would have to carry her beyond those swaying branches.

Why he should think of army discipline George did not know. The war had ended two years ago, but stories of marching men and the confidence discipline gave, came to him.

"Right foot forward now!" He almost shouted it, gripping her arm forcefully. "Right! Left! Right!"

He was fairly bellowing it out and she fell into step beside him until they had crossed directly under the tree. There, ahead of her, were the lights of her own house, not a quarter of a mile away.

"Don't shout," she said suddenly and almost crossly and he felt her arm relax. "What will people think?"

George wondered what they would think if they knew she still believed in ghost stories. It was the most ridiculous thing that had ever happened to him. But when he'd taken her to her own front porch and said a hurried "good night" he went home across the open fields. Somehow he didn't want to see the great horned owl in the half-leafed oak tree again that night.

Johannes was home when he got there. He was stretched out in a chair in the front yard, twanging on his banjo and humming snatches of songs to Bevy. The moonlight glistened on his shining hair, and his sharp, even features were etched against the dark stone of the house.

"So you took Elizabeth home," he said lightly. He was trying to sound natural but there was a sting in his voice.

"What else could I do?" George asked irritably. "Why weren't you here to take her yourself?"

Johannes didn't answer the question. "There's to be a Strouse dance in Lancaster next month," he said instead. "Maybe you can take her to that, too."

"Take her yourself," George snapped.

It was good that only Bevy was there to hear. He and Johannes were near a quarrel again, and this time over something positively silly.

10

A FORGE GLOWS IN THE NIGHT

This was the night.

For weeks Pep and George and Gid had worked on the wagons. The cross-members were mortised connecting the two sides, and the wide boards were secured by handmade wrought-iron clinch nails that had come from Gid's forge. They held tighter than rivets. Solid as though hewn from single giant logs were these two wagon bodies, now lying side by side in the grass in front of the wagon shop. Like huge, bright blue boats they glistened in the summer sun, and everyone who passed by had admired them. It would take the strength of two opposing Conestoga teams to tear the sides from those round-bellied bottoms.

These were Conestoga wagons!

Pep's eyes had shone with delight when each step had been finished. He had scarcely left George and Gid to make a move without his eagle eye observing each detail. Seldom had it been necessary for him to correct or advise, for George had learned well in the years past.

These wagons would be perfect.

"Now for the wheels!" Gid had cried when, with a whoop that brought him running, George had dragged the last of the doubletrees from the shade of the big tree overhanging the wagon shop. There he had been carving them out painstakingly for days, with the good hand axe Pep had given him long ago. He laid them neatly beside the spire-like wagon tongues which Gid already had plated with iron.

"George, and are you a wagonmaker! They'll last forever. Now for the wheels!"

"Four are finished," George said trying to keep the excitement out of his voice. Well Gid knew four were finished, for he had covered the tops and bottoms of those cone-shaped axles with close-fitting flat iron, days ago. He had measured the diameter and circumference of each wheel, cut the iron for the tires, beveled and welded it.

"The woodwork is worthy of your iron, Gid," Pep said wiping the sweat and dirt from his face, and George was proud. Pep did not give compliments unless they were deserved. In his mind George recalled the hours he had spent cutting the hubs to fit the axles, making the proper "dish" or concave hollow in the wheels, driving the spokes into the hub with a heavy mallet, each spoke meticulously gauged when it was placed.

"Tonight is the night," Gid had said almost under his breath, trying to appear calm. "Tonight I put the first iron tire on the first wheel."

"Shtuffle Henning will be here to lend a hand if need be?" George asked looking away, almost afraid to voice the question. The most intricate part of the wheelwright's work was shaping the axle and making the wheels with the proper "dish" to stand the strain of the road. Most dangerous and important of all was shrinking the iron tire onto the wheel.

"He'll be on hand," Gid answered. "But I'll be the blacksmith tonight and you'll be the helper." He smiled when he said it but the muscles in his throat were taut and his open shirt revealed his quickened breathing.

George looked toward the blacksmith shop where Shtuffle fanned the flames with his bellows. He was replacing a shoe on one of his own horses. His sure, skillful hands made no unnecessary move and under him Gid had learned well. But putting the iron rim on the new wheels. . . . All the hours of work George had done would be crowned or lost when that inch-thick iron tire, heated and glowing red, was placed on the wheel.

George did not mistrust Gid but he was glad Shtuffle Henning would be there, just as he had been glad more than once for Pep's quick "Tut! No, boy!" It had stayed his hand and saved re-cutting. He had seen Gid, with tools he himself had forged, remove loose tires from farm wagons, bevel and weld them to the circumference of the wood, and wield the heavy hammer to the hot iron until sparks flew against his apron and broadfall trousers of leather. Tonight George and Pep would add leather aprons to their clothing, for it took the quick work of more than one man to shrink a tire onto a wheel.

They sat in the shade and watched Shtuffle at his forge. The day's work was almost finished. No more horses would be brought for shoes today; no more wagons for repairs.

George ran his fingers over the smooth hubs and rims of his wheels, lying in the grass. The wood was almost soft to his touch, so carefully had he worked it. When the iron work was on, he would apply the paint. The red lead already had been ground and added, and it was waiting in the back of Pep's shop. He had decided not to paint until all four tires were on.

After that he would begin work on the wheels for the second wagon.

"Some day, Pep, we should change this wagon shop around." George said it more for conversation than because he really believed they would ever do it. And for conversation too, he guessed, his father asked, "How, George?"

With a stick George traced a plan he had in mind in the dirt, and Gid and Pep watched as though a real wagon shop was building before their eyes. Poplar boards at this end for bodies and tool boxes; next the hickory and gum for axles and hubs, and log butts for spokes; finally, white oak for tongues and doubletrees. Then the forge for ironing.

"Along here men would do the actual building. We would assemble a whole wagon under one roof." So George sketched in the space for his assembly line opposite the piles of lumber which his mind's eye saw, and the flaming forge that completed the picture—a forge where Gid held forth.

"That's something for you and Gid to do some day," Pep said looking beyond them to the blue hills that rimmed their valley. "You two—you know how, I believe."

Shtuffle Henning had finished with his horse. Soon the sun would drop behind the circling hills. Slowly George and Gid and Pep got up, watching while the animal was put to pasture.

"Which wheel, George?" Gid asked looking at the four that lay beside the assembled parts of their wagons.

"We'll take a front wheel tonight," George answered as easily as he could. If a wheel was to be lost, better it be a smaller one than one of the giant rear wheels that measured six feet in diameter.

They rolled it slowly toward the forge and waited while Gid, left hand on the bellows pole, rekindled the coals to a glowing red. Down the road from home George saw Grossedawdi coming with Jacob and Diederick behind him. Little had been said about this evening's task, yet many seemed to know that tonight Gid Hefs would iron the first wheel for George Bauman's wagon. The Showalter boys were coming too, and Johannes with them. It made George nervous, yet he would not have had any of them stay away.

From a half-dozen leather aprons that hung inside the blacksmith's shop Pep and George took down the uniform of the ancient trade. Silently Grossedawdi stepped to their side, took his apron, selected hammer and tongs with the others. Shtuffle was beside them now, his eyes squinted half shut, watching while Gid, tongs in his right hand, moved the heavy tire onto the stone blocks where wood already had been piled. A few coals from the forge, and the shavings and chunks ignited evenly all along the rim. The fire glowed into flame, condensed into red and amber heat.

George placed the wheel on the trestle and waited. It was Gid who would decide tonight when his iron was at the right heat; Gid who would give the signal. Not until he did would Shtuffle, Pep, and Grossedawdi move. Alert, like runners at the start of a race, they waited.

The iron changed color slowly. Slowly and evenly the heat expanded the tire. Every eye was on that great ring as it began to glow in the twilight, every man judging its expansion. Only Gid would decide the timing and George waited, bent and with tongs ready, anxious—almost frightened—for the word.

"Now! Altogether!"

Gid's voice was clear and sure. His angle tongs gripped the glowing red rim and at the same instant three others moved with him in unison. The iron circled the wheel and four hammers pounded it lustily into place. The clang of cold metal on hot iron was music; sweet music ringing like harness bells and echoing through the valley. Blows of small hammers and large hammers alternated rapidly and sparks flew against leather aprons and bare arms.

Before the wood could charr, while the wheel was still revolving, it was lowered into the trough of water with a whirr and spit and sizzle. Sudden cooling, uneven cooling, and the tire would break. Wait too long and the wood would be burned and damaged.

George could scarcely breathe. His throat and chest felt as though tongs gripped them too. The job of the helper was to use his heavy sledge now, for the shaping must be done before the iron became too cool. The job of the helper was to follow the signal of the blacksmith with blow after rhythmic blow.

George could not see Gid's eyes, for he dared not look up from the wheel, but he knew their glow of intensity when he gave the directions. None questioned him. A man scarcely had breath to speak now, until it was clear that the iron had shrunk tightly onto the wooden rim.

The hammering ceased at last. The sizzling of hot metal in cooling water slowly subsided. Men straightened up and wiped their faces dry of the sweat that ran down necks and backs and legs. As one they sighed with relief. In unison the Showalter boys walked to the blacksmith's water barrel to drink the drink that would make them as strong as he.

Deliberately Shtuffle Henning turned to Gid. "You are a man with a trade, Gideon Hefs," he said, and taking off his heavy apron, he walked back to his shop.

In the quiet that followed, George looked across the trough that separated him and his friend. Over their wheel, so surely made and safely rimmed, George and Gid shook hands.

11

STROUSE DANCE

After the night George and Gid had rimmed their first wagon wheel all the talk in the neighborhood was of the Strouse dance. Every evening when the young people gathered at the blacksmith shop to exchange news, somebody was sure to bring it up. Not until the fall schnitzing parties and corn huskings would there be another such affair.

Johannes, who had been in Lancaster, knew the most about it and he delighted in telling it, teasingly, a little at a time.

"It's to be very special this year," he said. "The aufscher is to be Henner Ritter, the storekeeper in Lancaster. It's to be upstairs over his store."

The country store everywhere was the social center and everyone knew Henner Ritter had a good store. Farmers took their home-grown and home-made produce there to exchange for salt and sugar, raisins and spices, or for the manufactured goods turned out in Philadelphia and the high-grade cotton cloth now coming into Pennsylvania from the textile mills in Rhode Island.

"I wish I could have a dress of some of the new materials," Bevy half pouted. "Elizabeth Yoder's going to have one."

"You know our mothers took their best homespun to the blue dyer in Lancaster weeks ago," Anna reminded her. "You'll have a new dress of that, same as me."

"There's to be material for a full suit for a lady given away, including bonnet and shoes and stockings," Johannes said looking knowingly at Anna and avoiding Elizabeth's eyes. "A nice prize for any girl's dowry."

"You should know all about it," George said in spite of himself. Why did Johannes direct his remark to Anna and ignore Elizabeth? Besides, Johannes had made two more unexplained trips to Lancaster and George was beginning to wonder about Elizabeth's hint as to his purpose. Even Pep looked as though he would like to know where Johannes went and why. Johannes never asked for a horse, even though it meant a long walk home unless he got a ride, and he offered no explanations. Remembering the nights at the inns along the road to Pittsburgh, George had thought perhaps his brother went for the riotous fun they offered, but Johannes never came home showing any sign of either fighting or drinking. No searching looks from Pep or hints from George brought the answer.

The Strouse dance was held on a warm Saturday night in July. All of the young people in the home neighborhood crowded into the Showalter wagon and there were more boys than girls. George thought Bevy and the Showalter boys were too young to go, but Anna had wanted everyone along, so they all went.

Johannes, again, was the one who knew best what they should do when they got there. He was in good humor, his dark eyes shining, and he sang snatches of some of the wagoners' songs to the delight of the Showalter boys and half-embarrassed giggles of the girls. He seemed particularly to want to tease Anna tonight.

"Each boy has to buy a ticket from the aufscher," Johannes explained. "You boys all have money, haven't you? That's what pays for the prize. After a boy buys a ticket he can take a girl into the dance, or go alone, as he pleases."

"Girls don't buy tickets do they?" Anna asked. She was crowded between George and Gid and she looked very pretty in her new blue dress, set off with a fancy kerchief and bonnet. Prettier, surely, than Elizabeth who had a dress of the new material her father had brought at Henner's store. George smiled down at Anna and felt a glow of pleasure at her appearance. It would be fun to dance with her again. They had been partners at all the neighborhood parties he could remember.

"Somebody'll buy you a ticket, Anna," George heard Johannes say knowingly. "Of that I'm sure."

"What about me?" Bevy asked, a touch of alarm in her voice.

There was a chorus of offers and George realized his little sister already was a very pretty young girl. The boys were noticing her heavy, waving light brown hair and shy, attractive ways.

Fireflies sparked in the yards of Lancaster, fragrance from summer flower gardens was sweet in the air, and weeping willows hanging low over the street swept the horses' necks. Laughter and excited voices and music greeted them when they drove into the yard beside the store and tied their horses at a post near dozens of other rigs. All together, for they felt strange in the pushing, noisy crowd, they made their way up the staircase on the outside of the building. Accordion, banjo, and fiddle tones came to them; the musicians were tuning up for the exciting dance. Inside the hall boys and girls crowded around a table in the center of the room where the prize was displayed. It was as Johannes had said; a fine gift for any girl.

Henner Ritter, a red-faced, apple-cheeked man, was tying a string around a candle which he placed in a lantern that hung above the table. To one end of the string a key was attached and he let the key drop through the lantern and dangle above the prize.

A chalk line extended from the table to the wall and George wondered what that had to do with the dance. He soon learned.

"Quiet now, everyone," Mr. Ritter called and the musicians ceased their scratchy tuning.

"I'll give this stick I have in my hand to the person at the chalkline after you all join hands and form a circle. A boy, a girl, a boy, a girl. When the music starts, the one who has the stick leads the dance around the hall to the chalkline again, then he hands it to his partner and she does likewise, each passing it on to the one behind after carrying it around the room once."

He paused to be sure they understood.

"When the candle finally burns down to the string and the key falls, the music will stop," he went on. "Whoever has the stick wins the strouse. If it is a gentleman, he gives it to his partner. If he brought no partner he gives it to the lady he would please. Now join hands, everyone, and the Strouse dance begins."

George looked to be sure Bevy was in the dance. The Showalter brothers each held her by a hand. He reached for Anna's hand and in that moment he saw Johannes turning from the room.

Johannes was not going to stay for the dance!

– 109 –

One of Elizabeth's hands was held by one Showalter brother. She reached the other for Johannes and she, too, saw him leave the room.

For one panicked moment George did not know what to do. He and Anna were next in the circle, then Gid who had no partner. Quickly George dropped Anna's hand and pushed Gid into his place. Gid followed George's eyes to the doorway through which Johannes had disappeared, then reached a hand each to Elizabeth and Anna and the dancing began.

Down the outside stairway George followed his brother. He would catch up with Johannes and demand to know why he was leaving Elizabeth alone at the dance and where he had been going all these nights when he had come to Lancaster. But to catch Johannes without shouting and attracting attention proved more difficult than George had anticipated. His brother slipped quickly through the clutter of wagons and almost ran down the tree-lined streets away from the center of town.

Before he had gone any distance at all George knew Johannes' destination. It was the wagoners' inn. Doors and windows were open there and the sound of music and revelry poured from this building too. For a moment Johannes stood, a black outline against the light, then another man came to the doorway and joined him. Together they walked away from the inn and George turned quickly not to be seen.

The man was big Lou Ludwig!

It would have been a simple matter to hide among the wagons and learn why Johannes had sought the wagoner out and George was tempted to do it. But that was something more dishonorable than he had ever done and George hurried back toward the dance, ashamed to have followed Johannes at all. These trips to Lancaster—they must all have been to make sure of a meeting with the powerful wagoner.

Big Lou Ludwig! If it had been Peter Weller, George could have understood. Peter Weller had offered to buy the Bauman grays. Had Ludwig made a better offer? He was a regular wagoner and he might well have bargained behind Weller's back for the horses that so nearly matched his own in strength and pulling power. Many regulars had more than one wagon. Christian Kline had three, George recalled, and his mind went back to his hazardous trip to Wheeling.

Johannes had no right to sell the grays, though. They were Pep's horses, not Johannes'. Could he actually have such a thing in mind?

Cautiously George slipped out of the inn yard and started back to town. What was his brother up to? Should he have stayed and tried to find out? Should he tell Pep the little he knew? Had he been right in following Johannes?

It was hard to know the right thing to do or what to think. Once before he had unjustly accused Johannes. He must not do that again.

George climbed the stairs to the hall over the store slowly. He had no heart for the Strouse dance now. The music was continuing, a monotonous sort of polka. Around and around the dancers went, always with the same step. Sitting on an empty bench by the door, George saw them through the haze of candlelight and smoke. He saw the key drop when the candle in the lantern finally burned through the string and with a start he realized the music had ended.

"The stick!" the aufscher called. "Who has it?"

"Here it is! I have it."

It was Gid Hefs' excited answer. "Here, I have it."

"And the lady-love of your choice?"

"Anna Showalter," Gid said in a good, clear voice.

George gave a sudden start and looked at the dancers again. They were crowding around Gid and Anna, clamoring and congratulating them. Gid's arm was around Anna's waist and he was leading her to the prize.

"What think you now, Brother George?" a voice behind him asked. It was the tantalizing, needling tone which George had not heard since the night at Ramsay's inn when Johannes had been drinking. It irritated him unreasonably but he choked back his anger and the retort he wanted to make.

At least Johannes had come back. He had not abandoned Elizabeth entirely. He could still dance with her and see her home.

12

THE PEACH TREES HAD BLOOMED
EARLY

The look on Anna's face had told George everything. Everything that others had been trying to tell him all summer. Gid had said they must have a talk but George had made no effort to see his friend alone. Elizabeth had hinted, Johannes had hinted, Anna had not come once to the Bauman house except with Elizabeth or her brothers, and she had not planned any summer festivity that would include George.

George sat on the bench and tried to realize that Anna was not his girl. She was Gid's girl. Sometime while he had been driving along the road to Pittsburgh or Wheeling, or while he was building his wagon or fretting over Johannes, Anna and Gid had fallen in love. Elizabeth had been right when she said things were different now that they were growing up.

But what about Johannes and Elizabeth? What about the plans he thought Pep had made for both himself and Johannes? And who was his girl, anyway?

Now that the Strouse dance was over the revelers were forming sets and straight fours and following the sing-song dance calling of Henner Ritter. George looked around the room. There were Lancaster girls here whom he had seen before. He would dance with them tonight.

George made it a point to wait at the forge the next night until all except Gid had gone. He sat in the grass, arms locked around his knees, and looked into the dying coals of the forge.

"Gid, when I came home from wagoning last spring you said there were things you had to tell me. I think I know what you had in mind."

He heard Gid draw a long breath and watched him stir the coals with his quick, almost nervous movements.

"Was it Anna?" George asked.

Gid tossed the pole aside and sat on the grass not far from George.

"It was Anna," he admitted. "But I have said nothing, George. To her or to anyone."

"Then you should."

"I am still an apprentice, for all Shtuffle Henning has favored me," Gid reminded him. "And I don't know what may have been arranged between your parents and hers."

"There may have been things said," George conceded. "I'm almost certain of it. But last night I saw the look on her face, Gid. Neither the Showalters nor Pep and Mem would go against her wishes. Most of all, myself."

"You're sure? Sure Mr. Showalter would take me instead of you?"

"Of course, if that's what Anna wants," George told him. "A good blacksmith is no mean fellow to have for a son-in-law, and you'll not come empty handed. Already you have your own wagon and next winter's work assured, to say nothing of your tools and the money Shtuffle will give you. He has no son. He should be generous."

"But you? What about you?" Gid persisted.

"I wish you well. Anna's a fine girl and you're lucky."

It was the only answer George could give. All the way home last night and all that day he had been thinking of that same question. It wasn't just that the plans he was sure Pep had made for a marriage between himself and Anna had gone awry. That day had seemed so far distant he had scarcely thought of it at all. It was the whole question of his future, and Johannes' too. What was Johannes scheming? It was Johannes who had forseen one of them should leave the valley. Surely it was clear now that he and not Johannes should go. What good could any deal with Big Lou come to?

So George's mind turned to Pittsburgh and Jennie Gilfillan. Only how little he knew about her. He had seen her but three times and he had not mentioned her to anyone here at home. Neither could he talk of her with Gid tonight, but the time had come to talk of Pittsburgh.

"Gid, I've about concluded that Pep's wagon shop is not for me, after all," George began slowly. "Pep needs but one helper, and one who has the farm at heart more than the shop. The only wagons built this summer were yours and mine. You know that."

"He has built for all in the valley," Gid admitted. "Another summer...."

"He has wheelwrights who need the work. They could have made our wheels."

"Then what will you do?"

"There's a man in Pittsburgh—a Mr. Wilkins. This winter when I go wagoning again I intend to talk to him. The industry for the great west country already is centering in Pittsburgh. There's boatbuilding where a woodworker could find employment and there are blacksmith shops where you could get work, if you had a mind. But there's no real wagon factory and I've been thinking...."

George had been thinking of the plan he had drawn in the dust and of what Pep had said: "That's something for you and Gid to do some day."

"You mean...?" Gid's voice was eager. Pep's words must have come back to him too. "Could we earn enough? Save enough?"

"We could earn and save and Mr. Wilkins could advise us well. How does it sound to you, if Pep is agreeable that I go?"

"Better than anything I ever dreamed of," Gid replied without hesitation. "Have you said anything to him?"

"Nothing, and until we've been to Pittsburgh and talked to Mr. Wilkins, I'll say nothing. But more and more I'm sure I'm the one to go and Johannes is the one to stay. Farming is right for him and with me gone..."

"You're an irritation to Johannes somehow," Gid admitted. "Where did he go last night? Did you find out?"

George told only the little he actually knew. He could not tell of the suspicion that disturbed him so greatly, not even to Gid.

"The more I think, the less I have to say," George concluded. "Why should Johannes not go to the wagoners' inn? No, Gid, I don't see how I can say anything to Pep, about my plans or Johannes' trips to Lancaster either."

They stared into the dying embers while the locust whirred in the trees above them with their endless summer chirping, and across the lowlands whip-poor-wills called.

George's mind was made up but it was not at ease. Six great, gray Lancaster horses grazed in the pasture below them. Horses no heavier or better bred had brought as much as

$1,000 each, George knew. With the price of six horses and a Conestoga wagon, Johannes could be very well established indeed, on a farm in Ohio.

Gid was looking at the horses too.

"Your Pep let me help break the young ones last winter," Gid told George. "They were two-and-one-half when we began working with them. Now they're ready for the summer's work and next winter's hauling and they know me as well as anybody."

Absent-mindedly George said yes. The young horses would justify Johannes, if there was any justification, in selling the grays. Pep and Grossedawdi would still have animals for the farm work; he and Gid would have them for their winter's work.

But the grays were not Johannes' horses, and what else would Lou Ludwig want?

George could not tell Gid what was on his mind. "You won't have any trouble with the young horses this winter," he said. "We'll all stay close together on the road though, you and Johannes and I. The bad places I'll tell you about before we start. It's safer if two or three wagoners stay together. There are some regulars we know now, too. A Peter Weller and Lou Ludwig. We might be able to follow along with one of them."

That was what they must do. There was just a chance George would learn of Johannes' plans that way.

Hot July days ripened the wheat and brought the harvest. Try as he would, George could not swing the cradle with the rhythmic skill Grossedawdi had so easily taught Johannes. Ahead of George those two cut the stubble to the same depth with each sure stroke, slipping the grain deftly out of the cradle and depositing it in even rows, no stalks sidewise or tangled. Behind the men, Mem and Bevy and Jacob, with wooden rakes, gathered the wheat and tied the bundles.

– 117 –

Apples ripened and were taken to the cider mill, or boiled in tremendous large iron kettles and spiced for apple butter. All day the apples were stirred over the open fire, with ladles on the end of ten-foot handles so the men could sit back in the shade of the trees and away from the merciless heat of the fires.

Tassels on the tall corn turned brown and husking bees finished off each farmer's harvest.

"Grossedawdi's husking bee comes Friday night," Pep finally announced at the supper table one night. "After the party you three can leave for Lancaster and on Saturday get your loads. Then Monday morning you'll be ready to start the winter's wagoning."

"Everybody'll be at the husking," Bevy said, her eyes shining. "It's the last big party of the year. Grossedawdi always has the best parties with the most food. I can hardly wait."

George, too, could hardly wait but it was not for the husking or the dancing or even the feasting. He was anxious now to be on his way to Pittsburgh. What had taken place there since he had promised Jennie Gilfillan he would come back? He had promised to go to Ohio, if that was necessary. How was he going to learn what Johannes might have promised he would do?

"It's best we start right after the party," George proposed. "There'll be no time left for sleeping that night."

"You can sleep Sunday after church," Pep proposed. "Gid, too. Shtuffle would no more have Gid haul on the Sabbath than I would. Pass the cream this way, George."

George looked across the table at Johannes, but his brother's eyes were on his plate. The summer's sun had browned his dark skin and the work in the fields had hardened his muscles. There was no softness about him anywhere. It was not unusual for him to eat in silence.

Friday brought a crowd of willing workers to Grossedawdi's big farm, with its lawns and barnyard more neat and orderly than ever. Grossememmi, "crazy clean" as always, had swept the barnyard and threshing floor and granary with the round splint broom Grossedawdi had made for her by shaving one end of a hickory pole into shreds. There wasn't even a spider web in the rafters.

The corn already had been hauled from shocks in the field to piles beside the barn. Inside the corn shed there were two huge cribs, one on either wall, and the space that separated them was wide enough for two wagons to drive through. There the corn was husked and there, work over, the dancing would take place.

It was a noisy, joking, frolicking crowd that gathered in two opposing rows with piles of corn between them, and vied to strip husks from ears and fill the crib behind them first. Everyone in the neighborhood was there, and the youngest girls and oldest men and women took part in the husking. The heavier job of carrying stalks in and out of the shed fell to George and Johannes, Pep and Grossedawdi, who worked as hard as the best of them.

"The first red ear!" the men began joshing. "Watch the girls to see who finds the first red ear!"

Whoever found the first red ear kissed her partner heartily. It was a game they always played and George had entered into it as merrily as the others in the years past, hoping Anna would be the one to find it. This year it was child's play to him and not until a shout went up, and Elizabeth was fairly lifted to her feet with a red ear gleaming in her tight hands, did George have any interest in it. He looked around for Johannes. At the far end of the shed, arms full of husks to take outside, Johannes was watching. His chin was set, his eyes half shut, while he waited.

But Elizabeth did not even look for Johannes. With only

a moment's hesitation she jumped across the piles of corn and kissed George lightly on the cheek, to shouts of delighted laughter.

George felt his face burn and his hands turn cold. He stood clumsily, wondering what to do. He couldn't laugh and swing Elizabeth around as was expected of him. He couldn't think of anything to say.

"Oh, George!" the Showalter boys laughed. "Are you afraid of girls? Stupid George!"

Everyone was laughing, even Grossedawdi.

"Give her a kiss!"

"Give her a whirl!"

George dropped the husks and spun Elizabeth around once then set her down beside her pile of unhusked ears. Why had she done this? It was practically an invitation for him to take her home. Everyone knew that.

George couldn't even look in Johannes' direction. Miserably his eyes sought Gid and the sober face he met told him that Gid, at least, understood his predicament. Then, following Gid's eyes to the open doorway he saw that Johannes had disappeared.

When the corn was husked the floor was cleared, first with the round splint broom then with the finer, flat corn broom. Lanterns and jack-o-lanterns were lighted and glowed cheerfully. Fiddlers, all in a group near one of the side doors, drew their bows and beat time with their feet, and lusty singing and clapping and calling followed their tunes. Colorful skirts swirled and sturdy boots stomped in rhythm on the plank floor of the corn shed.

George slipped outside and stood in the cool night air, wondering what to do. Where was Johannes? Had he gone home? George was about to slip down the tree-lined road and try to find his brother when he felt Pep's hand on his arm.

"What Elizabeth did was a foolish thing," Pep said quietly, "but you must mind your manners."

George moved farther from the lighted doorway into the shadows of the barnyard buildings.

"Pep, what am I to do?" he asked.

"If Johannes does not come back you'll have to take Elizabeth home," Pep said. " 'Twould disgrace us if you didn't and embarrass her before all the neighbors."

"But Johannes!" George protested. "Pep, you don't understand. There is always something between me and Johannes. This will be just one thing more."

"Maybe I understand a little," Pep suggested. "Anyway, there is no question of what you must do tonight. Now come back inside and join in the dancing."

"I have no heart to dance!"

"Then go help Grossememmie with the meats and salads and pies, but show yourself around."

George thought the dancing would never end. He tried to think of what he would say to Johannes when he finally got home. Wondered whether Johannes had gone home. There was no place else for him to go. Everyone for miles around was here at Grossedawdi's husking bee.

It was almost morning when the last of the food was cleared away and the rigs began taking the weary revelers home. George found Elizabeth and with all observing, he held her wrap for her and started down the little lane that separated the Yoder and Eschleman farms.

"You're angry with me, aren't you, George?" she asked when they were alone.

"Why did you do it?" George asked, trying not to be gruff, "You knew how it would make Johannes feel."

"What has Johannes cared about how I felt all summer?" Elizabeth demanded. Then, her voice suddenly soft and almost quivering, "Oh, George, don't you understand? Johannes had not paid any attention to me all summer, when everybody expected it. My parents. . . . Everyone. . . . I didn't know what to do."

George had not thought much about it, but it was true. Now that the words were said, Elizabeth poured out her story in little, jerking sentences.

"The swimming parties. He never came. I could understand why you didn't come after the Strouse dance. Then the schnitzing parties. . . . Why did Johannes stay away from everything?"

George did not know. They walked in silence for a little while.

"George?"

"Yes, Elizabeth."

"Who did Johannes see in Lancaster? You followed him that night. Don't you think I should know too?"

Her voice was pleading and beside him she seemed so thin and pathetic.

"It wasn't any girl, Elizabeth," George assured her, realizing he might have told her long ago. She, too, had seen Johannes leave the dance and she had seen George follow. She must have been wondering about it all these weeks. "He went to an inn and met a wagoner we both know," George explained.

A sigh escaped Elizabeth. "Even so, it's been plain he doesn't like me," she said. "And when I was unlucky enough to get that red ear tonight, what should I have done? Turn away from all the Baumans?"

George felt truly sorry for her. "It's all right, Elizabeth," he said, his voice gentle at last. "I don't know what's the matter with Johannes. When they call me stupid I think he's the stupid one."

He squeezed her hand reassuringly when he left her and

hurried home, more anxious and worried at the thought of meeting his brother than before. Why, indeed, had Johannes ignored Elizabeth all summer? Now it was time for him to go wagoning again and she would be alone all winter too, unless she discarded a Bauman for a likelier beau.

The light was burning in the kitchen when George came in, and Mem and Bevy were putting away plates of food they had brought home from the husking bee, but they were strangely silent. Was it just that they were tired or were they blaming him for the twist the evening's events had taken. He sat down wearily and watched them. Then Pep came in and Gid with him, and from their sober looks George was sure something had gone wrong.

"George, did you see Johannes tonight? After he left the corn shed?" Pep asked.

"No. Why?"

But before he asked it, George knew why. "He's gone! He's gone, hasn't he?"

Pep nodded. "He took his wagon and the grays and he's gone."

George got up and shoved his chair against the wall angrily. Without saying good-bye to Mem, or even to Bevy who loved him so greatly, without a word to Pep, Johannes had gone. Elizabeth and the red ear of corn had little or nothing to do with this. Johannes knew when Lou Ludwig would be in Lancaster next and he had arranged to meet him, beyond a doubt.

"Maybe . . . when we get to Lancaster . . ." Gid suggested but without conviction.

Pep shook his head and sighed heavily. "Perhaps you and Gid might as well get a night's sleep here at home," he said.

But they got no night's sleep.

Mem and Bevy went to bed leaving Pep and George and

Gid alone in the kitchen. Silently Pep filled his pipe and lit it with the candle. His heavy, rounded cheeks seemed to sag and George recalled how sober his voice had been when they talked together in Grossedawdi's barnyard after Johannes had left. How much had Pep suspected then? What might he know of Johannes' trips to Lancaster? Of his interest in a farm in Ohio? Should George tell him now of his own anxiety and of the worry he had not been able to throw off since the night he had learned why Johannes had kept going to Lancaster?

He had no time to decide the answer to those questions. A pounding at the kitchen door brought all three to their feet and before any one could speak Grossememmi staggered in. Her face was white and she could scarcely find breath to speak.

"Grossedawdi!" she gasped. "Grossedawdi!"

Pep half carried her to a chair, George and Gid helpless behind him. Grossedawdi had been at the husking all night, working and dancing with the best of them. Had it been too much for him?

"He's dead," Grossememmi whispered. "Sitting in his chair to take off his boots. . . ." She looked at Pep dully and clung to his strong hands.

Dead! Grossedawdi dead!

"The peach trees bloomed too early this spring," Gid whispered. "We all knew something would happen. I'll stay with you, George. When we go, we go together."

13

DAYS OF CHANGE

Gid kept his word. Soon after daylight he and George and Pep were ready for the work that must be done at Grossedawdi's big farm. Bevy had gone for Mrs. Showalter and Anna and Elizabeth who would help Mem and Grossememmi in the kitchen.

"Best we butcher two pigs as well as a steer," Pep directed. "We'll need at least thirty chickens too."

"I guess everybody in Lancaster County knew Grossedawdi," Gid said thoughtfully, looking up at the blessing stone over the door of the house. "He'd lived here all his life, hadn't he?"

Pep and George looked at the stone too. "*God bless this house what ere may befall it,*" the inscription read.

"Not all his life," Pep corrected. "He was born in what they call the Palentine section of Germany and he came to this country when he was fifteen years old as an indentured servant. You know what that means?"

"Like an apprentice?" Gid asked.

"No, it was harder than that," Pep told him. "A ship's captain would bring men who couldn't pay their own way. When they got here, employers who needed help would pay the captain the passage fee. A good man with a trade was worth fifteen English pounds in 1745 when Grossedawdi came. He had to give four years of service to the man who paid his way."

"They called the workers 'redemptionists' because they had to redeem their passage," George added. He knew the story of Grossedawdi's life well. It was Pep, though, who wanted to tell it.

"It wasn't the unskilled and uneducated who came, as you might think," he told Gid. "Conditions were bad in Europe then, and cold, hungry winters drove many good carpenters and masons and weavers and harnessmakers to leave their homes for America. Thousands came from the Upper Rhine villages and from Switzerland and even England and Ireland. Blacksmiths, saddlers, shoemakers. Grossedawdi had been a farmer and so it was a farmer who paid for him and brought him here to Lancaster County to work it off."

Gid looked from the barnyard to Grossedawdi's two-story stone house and the neat fields that surrounded it, and it wasn't hard to guess the question in his mind.

"He was thrifty, ya," Pep nodded. "And strong like George, and a worker. But he had a remarkable talent, too."

"Oh, I remember!" Gid agreed quickly. "A 'water smeller' they called him."

"By the twitching of the muscles of his legs he could tell when he passed over an underground stream," Pep explained, sharpening his knives while he talked. "In the days when Lancaster was being settled people would pay to find a well site. By the time he had completed his service he had enough money saved to buy the first of these acres."

"He never used a rod nor a witch hazel twig," George added with a touch of pride.

Grossedawdi was in his eighty-seventh year when he died and as Pep had expected, all the farmers in the valley and all the tradespeople he had known in his long life came to the funeral services. They stood outside the house, dead leaves from oaks and poplars falling on their good felt hats and best greatcoats, until the casket was carried out and placed in Pep's Conestoga wagon. They drove behind the family on the slow ride to the church and after they had heard the burial service and seen the polished wooden box lowered, they returned with Grossememmi and her family for the funeral feast.

This was the custom in the Conestoga valley.

It was not fitting that George should leave home for at least a week, and because Grossememmi took to her bed when it was all over, he and Gid did not leave for still another week. By that time it was certain she would recover.

Each day George groomed the horses. He was working with them in the barnyard when he and Pep actually said good-bye.

"They're good horses, George," Pep said looking from one animal to another. "Everything Grossedawdi did was well done, even to breeding his stock."

"And Gid has shod them well," George added. "There are few better on the road."

Pep ran his hands through the waving manes, stroked the strong shoulders.

"I've been thinking these last days," he began slowly. "Gid must set up shop some place where he will not be competing with Shtuffle. What's in his mind, George?"

For a moment George hesitated. Gid's plans and his own were so linked together that to tell of one was to include the other and when he looked into Pep's kindly inquiring eyes, he was sure the time had come. Leaning over the back of his favorite Sall, George told of the talks he had had with Gid; told again of Mr. Wilkins and the opportunities for work in Pittsburgh; told all except of the night he had followed Johannes to the wagoners' inn. It was easier than he had expected, for Pep interrupted only with an occasional "Ya."

"Since you were old enough to handle tools I've known you were the one to follow my trade," Pep said when George had finished. "I'd thought it would be here, in my shop, but I've lived to see times change. There are factories in Lancaster and in Reading now, where craftsmen work in one place instead of their own homes. It must be as you say in Pittsburgh."

It even seemed natural that Pep should know of the changes beyond the valley and George did not question it. "In Pittsburgh the workers don't even own their tools," he said. "Everything is in the factory."

"Ya," Pep nodded. "That's why I've been thinking I should give you at least part of your inheritance now," he said. "Owning the bays and your wagon, you can work for a time and save. Or you can sell the horses and start a small shop with Gid. Johannes and I can manage the farm with the grays he has and the young horses Gid will return to me in the spring."

For a few moments George could not answer. It wasn't just Pep's generosity. It was his expectance that Johannes would come home, when George doubted it so seriously. Why, Johannes didn't even know that Grossedawdi was gone, and if he went on to Ohio how was he to find out? Would he write, perhaps?

"Johannes is the farmer," George said and his voice sounded strangely husky, but he must reply to Pep.

"Johannes is my first-born, too," Pep replied soberly. "I shall give him the same share so he can plan too. This summer's foolishness must be forgotten. August Yoder and I have long known that Johannes was for the land and August has land too. So we have planned."

"Yes, Pep," George agreed. "Elizabeth would have it that way too. I know how she feels. There was no reason for Johannes to. . . ."

But Pep interrupted.

"When you see Johannes I want you to tell him what I have said. Tell him we all are waiting for him to come home. And I want you to try to put yourself in Johannes' place. Think back, to when you were little boys, and try to understand. Until you do, you and Johannes can never be as brothers should be."

It was not a rebuke. Pep did not say it in blame or fault-finding.

"When you grow up, George, you can no longer think as a child, the Good Book tells us," he added quietly. "You must try to assure Mem that Pittsburgh isn't as far away as she thinks, too. It's still in Pennsylvania, ya?"

He even laughed at his little joke, and leaning against Sall's sturdy flanks he clapped George on the shoulder with a firm, strong hand.

14

DANGEROUS PROMISE

Ruts and stones and branches that had fallen from overhanging trees bedevilled the road to Pittsburgh. Bad weather made driving slow and perilous and George and Gid slipped and slid along, covering no more than ten or twelve miles a day. George knew the road though, and warned of the hazards that might have delayed them even more. He felt like a seasoned wagoner, describing in advance the inns where food was best and stables cleanest, and cooks most generous with plates of food for the dogs.

"I should have thought Johannes would want Wasser," Gid said soon after they started. "Not that I'm sorry we are the ones to have him. He's almost like another person."

"The regulars seldom have dogs, and Johannes has made friends among them," George explained. "It's the farmers who take their dogs along. You'll learn the difference before you return home in the spring, taking the horses and Wasser back too, as we promised Pep."

Gid's dark eyes sparkled and he turned away to hide the smile that lightened his face at the mention of his return in the spring. He would be married then, and would bring Anna back to Pittsburgh to whatever home he and George managed to find for her this winter, if all went as they planned.

From the innkeepers along the road, George learned that Johannes was teaming with Lou Ludwig as he had suspected. They had gone to Pittsburgh two weeks ahead of George. From the innkeepers, too, he learned that Peter Weller was only a day ahead of him. That was good. He would be sure to see Weller at Ramsay's inn.

On the long, lonely miles George recalled his last talk with Pep, and often he tried to think what he should say to Johannes when they met. No matter what plan Johannes had in mind or what arrangement he had with Lou Ludwig, Johannes should return to the valley. George told himself he would try to understand his brother and listen to his reasoning when he learned what Johannes proposed to do, but all his trying ended only with an angry shake of the head, now. Johannes had not intended to team with him and Gid this winter. He had schemed all summer to meet Ludwig in Lancaster and get away from them. Why? Was he going to keep the grays, not knowing of Pep's generosity, and go on hauling as a regular? Those were questions that led to troublesome speculation, and finally to a grim decision. If Johannes would not go home, then George must give up his dream of Pittsburgh and return to the valley. Pep could not be left alone with the shop and the farm until Jacob and little Diederick were old enough to help. Pep could not be abandoned by both of his grown sons.

"Shouldn't we be meeting Johannes soon?" Gid asked when at last they reached a point less than a week distant from Pittsburgh. "I thought he'd be on his way back to Philadelphia with a load, by now."

They were feeding their horses at the Black Crow, a dismal

place, and George had no relish for it, but night had overtaken them there. Once more they both had scanned the inn yard for Johannes' wagon and had not found it.

"I'll ask again tonight," George said but he dreaded asking. If Johannes had not been seen here either, it was almost certain he had not taken a load for Philadelphia. Had he gone on to Wheeling? Was he already on his way to a farm in Ohio? George kept the disturbing questions to himself. There would be time enough to talk to Gid when the facts were known.

That night they both learned the story. Among the wagoners at the Black Crow was Peter Weller.

"George Bauman!" The big, balding man shouted his name as soon as George and Gid entered the crowded inn. "Come! Come over here!"

With Gid following, George pushed through to Peter Weller's table while Weller pounded with his mug signalling for more food. They drew a small bench to a place beside him. The air was heavy with the smoke of many "stogies" and the odor of pork and cabbage, the room warm from the uneven heat of an open fireplace.

"I thought you were a day ahead of me at least," George said. "Maybe more, for you often haul steadily without resting the seventh day." He had to shout to be heard above the din in the room.

"I'd have been in Pittsburgh now, but for an accident that wrecked a front wheel," Weller explained. "There's a wheelwright here but he's immortal slow. I've sat three days now, watching him hack out a few spokes. But in the morning I'll start with you."

"Three days," George repeated. Weller was sure to know of every wagon that had passed in either direction during those days. George moved closer to the wagoner. "Have you seen Johannes?" he asked.

"I've not seen him, no," Weller answered. He looked up from his well-filled plate to peer at George questioningly. Then, lowering his voice, "You know where he is, don't you?"

George felt his heart pounding unreasonably. Something in the hushed tone told him Johannes was not returning on the road to Philadelphia.

"Where?"

Weller hesitated, moving his head slightly in Gid's direction.

"Gideon Hefs is my partner. Anything you know he can know," George said.

"Johannes is with Lou, headed for the National Pike," Weller said directing his attention to his plate again. "Lou's been taken in with this talk of Wheeling outstripping Pittsburgh. He thinks there's more business and more can be charged for hauling on the new road. There's no toll to pay because it was built with Union funds. This past August, the first United States Mail passed over it, too. But Pennsylvania'll have its road finished before long now."

George heard Gid let out a long breath. He, himself, had almost forgotten about the rivalry between the two cities and the conflict over the roads, and it was news to Gid who began questioning Weller about it now.

George let them talk. Before his half-shut eyes the rough road to Wheeling curved and twisted. Even if he had made no promise to Jennie Gilfillan, even if her father had come for her as he hoped to learn, there was no alternative now.

It was mid-afternoon when George and Gid and Weller drove into the yard at Ramsay's inn. Here was the rutted sea of cobblestones and mud that George remembered. Hens cackled, pigs snorted, and yipping dogs chased them both. At the forge, hammers rang on hot iron. Wagoners who were resting their teams between hauls greased axles or tightened chains, noisily calling to each other and shouting in endless arguments.

Almost furtively George looked from the kitchen to the hen houses, but there was no sign of Jennie Gilfillan. He let Weller and Gid unharness faster and take their horses to water first, and he held back when they started for the inn saying he would be with them in a minute. When they were safely inside, he went to the kitchen door.

Now that he was there at last, George felt strangely calm. It was a pleasure to think of the scene in the kitchen when he opened the door. He could picture the anxious look, then the light of recognition in the green eyes he remembered so well.

He knocked, then opened the door without bidding. The November sunshine had been bright and the kitchen was dimly lit, but even before his eyes adjusted to the change George knew something was wrong. This was not Mary bent over the table. George blinked again, and looked into the round faces of two Negro women. For a moment he was speechless and the women stared at him in equal surprise.

"Where . . . where's Mary?" George stammered. "Where's Jennie Gilfillan?"

"Who? Who's they?"

"Mary was the cook," George explained. "Where is she?" Then, as alarm replaced surprise, "*Where are they?*"

"We dunno," one of the two told him, wiping her flour-covered hands on her apron.

"How long have you been here?" George did not mean to be cross, but here was a situation he had not anticipated.

"We bin here a week," one of the two answered reluctantly. "But don't look at us like we wuz run-aways. We got our papers. Boss man seen 'em."

George had not thought of accusing the women of being run-away slaves. At the reference to Ramsay he looked instinctively across the kitchen toward the entrance to the inn.

How long Jim Ramsay had been standing there, back to the wall, George did not know. When George saw him he started across the kitchen. The slouched, unconcerned walk, the expressionless face had not changed.

"Come on in, George," he said easily. "What delayed you?"

"Delayed me?" George repeated. "Why ... who ..."

"Johannes said you were two days behind him. It's been two weeks."

Ramsay was looking at him intently, his eyes sharp. Something in that look, something in the posture, put George on guard.

"Where's Johannes?" he asked instead of answering the question. Through his mind flashed the remembrance that no one here except Gid knew why he had been delayed. He had said nothing to Peter Weller of Grossedawdi's death. No one knew of the inheritance Pep was giving Johannes and himself. He must get to Gid and make certain nothing was said; that no word of it reached Johannes until he could tell it himself, and give Pep's message to his brother as Pep wanted it told.

Why was Ramsay questioning him about the delay, George wondered. There was more here than idle curiosity.

"You don't know where Johannes is?" The tone indicated plainly that Ramsay did not believe him. The innkeeper had come across the kitchen and was standing with his back to the one window so the light fell directly upon George.

"You ask me where Johannes is! I ask you where Jennie Gilfillan is." Ramsay spoke slowly, his voice thick and his eyes intent upon George's face.

For a moment George was too shocked to reply. Could it be that Ramsay did not know where Jennie had gone?

"You mean . . . you don't know?" George stammered in alarm.

He heard Ramsay draw a long breath. "Nor do you, I see."

"You thought. . . ." It was George who moved menacingly, closer to the window where he might see the expression on the other's face clearly. "What did you think? And when did she go?"

She went a week ago, and Mary with her," Ramsay answered directly. "Johannes said you were two days behind him. I thought. . . ."

He turned away as though to leave the sentence unfinished but George stepped in front of him, blocking the way.

"What did you think?" he demanded.

"That it had been pre-arranged, probably through Johannes," Ramsay said bluntly. "I thought she had gone to join you somewhere."

Clearly Ramsay knew now his guess had been wrong. The probing look in his eyes had faded, the lines in his face deepened.

"They could have gone to Wheeling with Johannes and Ludwig," he said, more to himself than to George. "Not once did I see Johannes talking to her, or even near the kitchen." Then, his mind returning to George, "Why were you two weeks behind Johannes?"

George was not certain what to say, but the conviction that he should not tell of Grossedawdi's death grew stronger.

"Weller had an accident. A broken wheel. And we had bad weather and this was Gid Hefs' first trip. We were slow."

Ramsay could check on all this he knew, but it was true. George followed him when he started toward the big room of the inn. He was not through talking to the innkeeper.

"As soon as my horses rest I'll be ready to take another load of nails to Wheeling, Ramsay," George said deliberately. "Are you still looking for men who'll risk bringing out your furs?"

Ramsay stopped short and stood staring at the orderly rows

of barrels and boxes, the cupboards of food and dishes in his kitchen. When he finally answered his voice was bitter and his eyes again were peering as though to fathom George's mind.

"I'm looking for a man to find Gilfillan!"

George met the searching look without flinching. "I'm looking for Gilfillan too," he said.

"Why you?"

"I, because I think him innocent. You because you think him guilty, but both of us because Jennie must have gone to him somehow," George replied.

In the dark, smoke-tinged room, where two unconcerned Negro women stirred at iron kettles filled with stewing chickens and shuffled apple pies in and out of huge ovens, George and Jim Ramsay faced each other once more. It was Ramsay who finally looked away.

"Whoever is right, I must know no harm has come to the girl," Ramsay said at last.

George did not reply. He had a promise to keep—a promise he had made to Jennie. And he must find Johannes. He waited for Ramsay.

"Will this Gid Hefs go with you?" the innkeeper asked cautiously.

"I think Gid will go if I ask it, he is tough and reliable," George said. "Weller...."

"Weller will go," Ramsay told him, his eyes narrowing.

"How can you be so sure?" George asked. "Weller told me business was good enough for him on the Conestoga Road."

"Weller will go," the Scot repeated. There was a knowing look on his face and he turned abruptly toward the door leading to the inn. "There will be nails for three loads to Wheeling."

15

PROUD MISSION

After the shouting and singing and dancing were over and the men lay snoring on the floor, Ramsay led George and Gid and Peter Weller to his kitchen. He lit two candles and set them in the center of a heavy saw-horse work table, and with a gesture motioned the three to a bench beside it. The flickering light threw eerie shadows against the wall and dying logs in the fireplace crackled and spluttered in the strange silence.

The Negro women had scrubbed the work table clean, piled boxes and barrels in orderly rows against the wall, stacked kettles and baking dishes neatly in the cupboards. Even Mary had kept the kitchen no better.

It was Ramsay who had told the three he would see them tonight, and not even George knew what he would say or what proposition he would make. In a hurried conversation with Gid that afternoon George had made his one request.

"Ramsay knows Johannes has gone to the National Pike," George reported. "He doesn't know I must find him, or why.

I don't want anyone here to know of Grossedawdi's death, or that I own my horses and wagon, until I find Johannes."

Gid looked at George questioningly. "Anyone would be proud to own a Conestoga wagon and six horses," he hazarded.

"Let's hear what Ramsay has to say," was the only answer George gave. "I would keep my business with Johannes between you and me, until we find him."

Now, in the quiet midnight, Ramsay drew a chair to the table and came quickly to the point.

"It's no secret that I have been engaged in the fur business for years," he began, looking at the candles instead of the men. "Not only do I profit from it, but so do others in Pennsylvania. The merchants who buy them, the people who finally make use of them. Everything that comes out of the new west country into Pennsylvania profits someone here. The wagoners too."

He stopped and looked from one to another, his eyes finally resting on Gid.

"This is your first trip," he said. "You get a wage for hauling and so do all wagoners, but there's more to it than that. You can get a wage for hauling on the National Pike too. You can take the grain and hides and smoked meats from Ohio and Kentucky away from Pennsylvania if you want to. You can deliver the goods to Baltimore instead of Pittsburgh and Philadelphia and do just as well for yourself."

"Why would a Pennsylvania man do that?" Gid asked.

"That's for Pennsylvania men to decide," Ramsay replied. "I could close my inn here and go to Wheeling. I could sell furs in Baltimore. Those of us who have always lived here, who believe Pittsburgh will win in this struggle with Wheeling, we will stay here and fight."

George felt his cheeks grow hot while Ramsay talked. Johannes had gone with Lou Ludwig to haul the raw products from the west away from Pennsylvania. Ramsay knew it and so did Weller and Gid.

"It's no secret," he heard the innkeeper saying, "there has been thieving, and loads intended for Pittsburgh never got here. George has told you both of his experience, no doubt. But it's more than just my loss. I want to get the men who schemed it all, and stop it. Not to get my furs through alone, but to make the roads safe for wagoners who are men enough to make the Wheeling trip in the winter when the river is closed. The business must keep coming through to Pittsburgh."

In the quiet that followed, George could almost hear his heart pounding. Even if he did not have reasons of his own for going to Wheeling, Ramsay had thrown out a challenge. The Scot was sure of George, as well he knew. Would Gid and Weller be carried along with this appeal for loyalty to Pennsylvania?

Cautiously George looked up from the burning candles. Weller and Gid and Ramsay himself were watching the melting wax trickle, slowly, lumpily, down the pillars of tallow. Finally Ramsay spoke again.

"In the case of my furs, one of two men is responsible. I think of one, George of another. Isn't that so, George?"

George looked at Ramsay quickly. How did he know George suspected McKeeb, not Gilfillan? But he was right. Those two always knew when the furs came into Wheeling. McKeeb, at least, always knew when and how they left, and perhaps Gilfillan did too. George nodded in agreement.

"George is ready to make another trip to Wheeling. We both have reason for wanting to locate the man I bargained with originally for the furs. If he can be found . . . if I can face him. . . ."

Ramsay left the sentence unfinished. He had not mentioned the danger but there was no need to. He had not even offered an inducement of any kind to Gid and Weller for making the perilous journey and George waited, wondering if he would not. Weller knew Ramsay paid well, and that he had a reputation for choosing only the most reliable wagoners for his business. There was recognition in his selection of a wagoner. But all of this was new to Gid and no one could blame him if he hesitated to go on so dangerous a trip.

Ramsay was not through talking however.

"In two days, November 21st to be exact, the Monongahela Bridge Company completes the last arch and lays the last flooring of the great bridge that now crosses the river," he told them. "Tomorrow you must go and see it. It's a spectacle like nothing else in the country. Fifteen hundred feet long and built at a cost of $102,000."

It was the bridge Mr. Wilkins had told about last winter; the bridge that would cut into Ramsay's income from his ferry and George was surprised to hear him mention it.

"There'll be a magnificent celebration," Ramsay told them. "A parade is planned and a dinner'll be served to the workmen right out on the bridge, with dignitaries making speeches. The tables and food are all arranged for. A cannon's been placed on the middle pier and it will be discharged when the last plank is down. That's when the celebration starts. That, too, is our defiance of Wheeling and our statement of faith in Pittsburgh."

Ramsay was leaning over the table, closer to the lighted candles, and his face had taken on an intensity George had never seen before.

"When the speech-making and music and dancing are over, and after the gold-plated coaches have crossed the bridge, then the first commerce will start. The first wagoners, with horses and harnesses shining and bells in tune and gleaming, will cross the bridge. I've arranged for George to be one of them. I can arrange for you, too. But if you do it, you must be aware of the danger as well as the glory."

George stared at Ramsay in amazement, then turned to Gid, meeting his friend's surprised and questioning eyes with a look of equal surprise. Across the table Weller was wiping beads of sweat from his forehead.

"Liewer Gott!" the wagoner whispered.

"It's an honor that comes to few," Ramsay said and George sensed that now the Scot was talking to Weller alone. "Lou Ludwig's never hauled for me, nor will his name be known as one of the first to cross the Monongahela Bridge. He should be brought back though, to carry the commerce down the Pennsylvania road!"

George had seen men play for high stakes, seen them match strength and endurance, but never had he seen a struggle such as this. Ramsay wanted Weller! Wanted him more than he wanted George or Gid to make this trip to Wheeling but he would not say it; would not ask. He had been gambling when he said Weller would make the trip. He had one more card to play, and he played it now.

"It is my own feeling that a seasoned man, known and respected among the wagoners, should lead the procession. George is young . . . so is Gid, if he decides to go. But whoever makes this first trip across the bridge to Wheeling for me, must know full well his is a dangerous mission as well as a proud one."

Weller got up at last. He did not answer Ramsay but turned directly to George.

"You intend to go, George," Weller said. "I can see that you would want to bring Johannes back. I would rather have Johannes and those powerful grays with me than with Lou Ludwig—a point you didn't make, Ramsay, ya? But no matter."

He paused and wiped his forehead again, then went on without glancing at the innkeeper.

"What I want to know of you, George, is why you should be concerned with this man that Ramsay deals with?"

The question came so suddenly, so unexpectedly, that George could scarcely realize he had been confronted with it. He had not told Gid nor anyone else of Jennie Gilfillan or his promise to her. There was no answer now but an honest one. If they were to undertake this mission together, certainly there should be understanding and confidence among them all. Slowly George slid from the bench and got to his feet to face Weller.

"The man Ramsay suspects and wants to find is Robert Gilfillan," George said hoarsely. "I believe him innocent, and I promised his daughter I would go back to Wheeling this winter and try to find him for her."

"The girl!" Weller said under his breath. "A little red-haired girl only a year or two ago. Now she'd be. . . ." He looked at George and nodded knowingly. "I remember her now. Where is she?"

George turned to Ramsay. Let him tell it.

"She's gone," the innkeeper said and his shoulders slumped when he said it. "Neither George nor I know where, but we think to her father. That's our business though. It should not have any bearing on your decision."

Gid pulled the bench from the table, straddled it easily and got to his feet. George's temples pounded while he waited to hear what his friend would say, now that he knew all. It was a moment before Gid found his voice.

"I go with George, of course," he said simply. "I would not be left out."

They stood then, shoulder to shoulder, looking down at Ramsay and waiting for Weller.

"You win, Ramsay," the wagoner finally said. "It's a proud mission for three Pennsylvania Dutchmen, ya?"

16

THE CRY OF A WOLF

George stood with Gid and Peter Weller beside the poplars and stared at the miracle bridge that spanned the giant Monongahela, but his mind was not on the spectacle or the celebration. Like thunderheads moving in over the Conestoga hills came the picture of Zane's Trace cutting the dark, snow-covered forests beyond Wheeling. There was no turning back now from the tasks he had taken upon himself and there must be no failure. His dream for the future, Pep's hope for Johannes' return, Jennie's fate, even the destiny of Pittsburgh itself, all would be forged in the days and weeks ahead.

"That entrance now, it's something like the covered bridges back Lancaster way, ya?" George heard Weller observe.

Soon they would drive their wagons through those yawning portals into the covered entrance and thence out onto the ribbon of planks that crossed the river.

"If I wasn't seeing it with my own eyes I wouldn't believe

it," Gid fairly gasped. "The engineers must know, but you can't help wondering. . . . Well, they must know it will hold the weight."

"Stone piers it's got," Weller said reassuringly. "Seven between the abutments. . . ."

The booming of a cannon interrupted him and at the signal the City Guards of Pittsburgh marched out onto the bridge, and from the village of Birmingham on the south side of the river another group of uniformed men started marching. They passed at the central arch where a United States flag was waving, and there they paused to fire salutes.

"Wheeling has nothing like this," George declared. "Let's get closer and hear what's being said."

He was thinking that perhaps Mr. Wilkins would be among the dignitaries at the ceremony. Twice George had gone to the bank to see him but both times the banker had been busy with arrangements for the celebration, or was with important people who were his guests for this historic occasion. It had been disappointing because he had told Gid they would see Mr. Wilkins when they reached Pittsburgh. Now, crowding nearer, he tried to find his friend among the distinguished people at the tables where the workmen were being honored. He strained his ears to hear the toasts:

"To the State of Pennsylvania, first in the Union for the number and beauty of its bridges!"

The applause was tremendous. These were Pennsylvanians who believed in their state. They toasted their legislature and their governor next and the crowd cheered. They paid a less thunderous tribute to the President of the United States and dutifully mentioned the 16th Congress before honoring their own civic leaders. At last came the final toast:

"The President of the Monongahela Bridge Company, distinguished for his public spirit!" The spokesman shouted the words triumphantly and George pushed Gid forward.

"That will be Mr. Wilkins," he said. "Look! There he is! That's the man we'll see when we get back to Pittsburgh. It's plain he couldn't have seen us now."

They stood on tiptoe and stretched their necks for a glimpse of him when he rose to acknowledge the honor.

"It's all as Ramsay said it would be," Weller observed pushing the big felt hat back on his head so it framed his round face. "You can't but respect the man."

George would have been the last to contradict it, but there were reservations in his mind. Ramsay must have made Jennie Gilfillan increasingly uncomfortable under his roof, or she would not have undertaken the hazardous and dubious trip to Wheeling, with no money and no certainty of finding her father when she got there. But where else had she gone? Had Mary gone with her? Would she have dared go alone?

It was Jennie, almost as much as Pep and the family at home, who was on his mind while he waited to drive across the bridge behind Peter Weller. Gid was third in line. This was a moment of pride for them all and George wished someone who knew him could have been there to witness it. If Pep could only know that two of his teams were among the first to cross. If Pep knew all—everything this trip to Wheeling meant —he would have told George to go, he was sure.

Ahead George saw Weller talking to his horses, giving them lumps of brown sugar, inspecting the polished harnesses. George dismounted to walk beside his own teams, dividing apples, slapping the strong necks, stroking Sall's soft nose. It would never do to have them alarmed or out of control when they drove from the entrance out onto the open span that crossed the high-flowing river.

George had thought he would be able to look at the people on the banks, but his whole attention was on the horses when he followed Weller through the covered section of the bridge. At the open span, where so short a time before tables had been stretched for dining and speech-making, Barney shook his dark mane, held back and stopped, pulling his companion to a halt with him. Never had the animals balked, but the excitement, the strangeness of the bridge, the rushing water below were new and frightening.

"Now Barney. Easy now."

George tried to sound reassuring but there was danger here. The horses must have time to get accustomed to the heavy wooden planks beneath their feet, the rosin smell of fresh lumber, the sound of the river. Peering from the dimness into the November sunlight ahead, George saw Weller driving straight down the center of the bridge. How had he managed his horses so surely? Had they crossed bridges like this before? Weller's wagon was old and the paint chipped off; he and Gid had new wagons and none more finely built or more gaily painted, but it was the old wagoner who drove with assurance out onto the bridge that was Pittsburgh's pride. Ramsay had judged right.

He thought of Gid behind him. Gid was being held up, but Barney was still pushing back against Sall, jerking at the lead line, stepping nervously from side to side and switching his long tail.

"Easy, Barney! Nothing's going to hurt you."

One flighty horse could agitate the other five and Barney's snorts and heavy breathing were alarming. Six frightened animals, plunging across the bridge, might hurl the wagon, themselves and the driver into the river. And six tons of weight would carry them all down to death.

George ran his hand along Bill's neck and spoke again. The wheel horses were still as monuments.

"Sall, old girl?"

She lifted her head when he called her name, and stood still. George breathed easier. Sall was not nervous.

Weller had almost reached the middle arch before Barney quieted and George risked driving onto the open bridge.

"Ready, Barney?"

He waited a moment then pulled on the lead line. "Gid-dap!"

For an instant George thought the horses were not going to move but he dared not risk the whip.

"Barney!"

There was authority in his voice and he gave the lead line a firm jerk. His knees pressed against Bill's flanks and the wheel horses started. The wagon tongue prodded the middle team and at Sall's first step the lead team responded.

George leaned forward to urge them on. His head pounded and his throat was dry but he had his horses under control.

Bright with red and blue paint, black iron work shining, harness bells chiming harmoniously, the new Conestoga wagon moved majestically onto the great bridge. George measured the distance on either side and guided the way down the center. Ramsay, or Mr. Wilkins himself, might be on the bank watching. They must see a wagoner in command of team and load.

Gid too. George dared not turn his head to look but his ears soon told him Gid had used this time well and his horses were unafraid. Tinkling bells and iron shod hooves pounding the planks behind, answered for Gid.

Gid always had answered well for himself, George thought. He followed surely across the bridge and on the long trip down to Wheeling, George learned to value his friend's quick thinking more than ever. It was Gid whose cautious, guarded questioning at the inns assured them Johannes and Ludwig carried no passengers with them on the trip to Wheeling.

Gid was the one, too, who was thinking of how they should proceed if all did not happen as Ramsay had forseen and what they should do if they could not follow the strategy Ramsay had mapped out. It was his zealous planning for their future together, his thrifty schemes for managing time and money once they were started on a business of their own, that made the thought of failing hurt. George would find Gilfillan no matter how long it took or how far into Ohio he had to travel, but if he could not persuade Johannes to return home with the grays, then there was no side-stepping his own responsibility.

Ramsay's first planning went awry when they were less than three days from Wheeling.

"Don't tell McKeeb you're looking for Gilfillan," Ramsay had directed. "You are looking for Lou and Johannes. Get loads for Zanesville, and once beyond Wheeling, start asking questions. Gilfillan's known. For more than five years he's been bringing furs to McKeeb's post for me," Ramsay had said.

In the dark hours before dawn, while feeding their horses and preparing to start from the inn as soon as daylight came, George and Gid were talking of the snow that had fallen in the night, of the trouble to expect on the road, and finally of Ramsay.

"He's probably right in advising us to tell Gilfillan it's a new business arrangement that must be made," George said thoughtfully. "The Scots are as thrifty as the Pennsylvania Dutch. But it's not what's on my mind and. . . ."

The cold air suddenly echoed with an anguished animal

cry. One howl, long drawn out, rising and falling—a cry of pain. It was startling and blood-chilling and George and Gid both turned toward the woods beyond the inn and listened.

"A wolf," George said. "Those woods must be full of them. I saw a few yesterday."

"A wolf caught in a trap!" Gid touched George's elbow. "Listen!"

The very sound hurt. Unquestionably the wolf had been injured and most probably caught in a trap. This was not the snarling cry of a fight.

Gid's voice dropped almost to a whisper. "Let's get our rifles."

"Why? We should be starting soon. There'll be no wolves on the road."

"Where there're traps there are trappers," Gid replied. "That trap isn't far distant, either. Who knows what we might discover."

Still George hesitated.

"Blacksmiths know of other smiths for miles in all directions," Gid pressed. "Wagonmakers know of those in their same trade, so why not trappers?"

It was a possibility. With a word to Weller they started into the black woods, moving cautiously, watching for gleaming eyes, guided first by the low, whining sounds then by a dull metallic pounding that told them the wolf was trying to free himself by beating the trap against a tree. Failing in that, he might bite off his own foot. George had heard stories of the early days when animals were trapped in the woods at home and along the Conestoga Creek. An injured animal could be vicious. George moved slowly, watching and listening with every step and grateful for the snow which had buried dry leaves and fallen twigs.

Then with a suddenness that stopped them short, crashing

branches to their left told them they were not alone. Man or animal, something was hurrying through the woods and soon was ahead of them. Something not afraid and cautious as they had been. George clutched his rifle tighter and waited, Gid close behind him. After a few seconds they moved forward slowly following the sounds until, almost as though they had expected it, a rifle shot rang out and echoed . . . the shriek of a dying animal . . . another shot.

Gid had been right. Traps meant trappers. George hurried ahead, calling out so they would not be mistaken for prowling animals.

"Where are you?" George shouted.

The answer brought him up short.

"Here at your elbow. Who might you be and what do you want?" It could have been Ramsay himself, so thick was the Scottish burr.

Stepping from the shadow of a tree into a patch of snow George saw the silhouette of a tall, thin figure, the wolf a black object hanging from the trap held in his hand.

"When we heard the wolf cry we thought if the trapper was near by, he'd come," George began to explain.

"It was the trapper you wanted to see, not the pelt?"

It hadn't occurred to George they might be accused of trying to rob traps, nor probably to Gid either. They hadn't had time to think of this eventuality.

"It was the trapper," George insisted. "There's a man we must find and one in the business of trapping might know of others."

"Name him, then."

The man towered above George. His voice was commanding and hard with disbelief. Dropping the trap he came closer. In the graying light George saw a fur cap pulled low over forehead and ears, and a heavy beard covering cheeks and chin, but the features were barely discernible.

George gave his answer quickly. "His name is Robert Gilfillan."

For long, slow seconds George waited. Why was there no answer? Either this man had heard of Gilfillan or he had not. At last George knew. The words were cautiously spoken, cold and unfriendly.

"I'm Gilfillan. Who are you? What do you want?"

Gid might have been anticipating this too, but George had not. Ramsay and all he had advised were forgotten.

"I want to know where Jennie is!" George demanded. "Did she come to you? Where is she?"

"Jennie!" It was the trapper who was taken by surprise. "Jennie? My little lass?"

He was fairly upon George, one hand raised as though to strike.

"What are you saying?" Gilfillan demanded. "Who are you and what do you know about Jennie?"

"If you're Robert Gilfillan, she's your daughter. But she isn't back in Pittsburgh where you left her. Where is she?"

The hand lowered slowly and the man bent nearer trying to see George's face. It was as though he, like the wolf, had one moment been free in the forest, self-assured in his own strength, then caught in the iron claws of a trap he had not known was there.

"Not in Pittsburgh? Who are you and what are you saying?"

"I'm George Bauman and this is my friend Gid Hefs. Didn't you get the message I left for you last winter? Didn't you know Jennie sent word to you that Mrs. Ramsay had died?"

It was George who was commanding now, George who was trying to judge a strange face in the first light of morning.

"Message? Mrs. Ramsay dead? . . . Where did you leave such a message? With McKeeb?"

The words were stumbling, the voice incredulous, but this *was* Gilfillan and he, too, wanted the truth.

George told him everything. The forest blackness turned to gray mist and in the dawn-light of a new day George saw deep-set blue eyes, heavily lined and hollow cheeks, a square chin. Pride and determination were Jennie Gilfillan's heritage.

At first the trapper listened open-eyed and breathing heavily. Slowly the eyes narrowed and a look of shrewdness, not unlike Ramsay's own expression, came over his face.

"You, George Bauman, you believe what Ramsay told you?"

"I know," George said. "I was there and Jennie was gone. I myself was robbed last winter."

Automatically Gilfillan released the carcass of the wolf and unclamped the chain on his trap.

"Are you afraid to take out another load of furs?" he asked.

17

JOHANNES BAUMAN

All was not working out as Ramsay had planned but better, George thought. Ramsay had not asked the wagoners to risk bringing another load of furs up from Wheeling. He would pay them well if they did it, but he had left that decision to them. All he wanted was that they find Gilfillan and bring him back.

Gilfillan would trap the thieves too. In no other way could he clear his name, face Ramsay with proof, justify Jennie's faith in him and unashamedly search until he found her.

Gilfillan did not expect she would be in Wheeling. It was agreed George should go to Zane's tavern, and watch the streets and market places, but Jennie's father thought she would be somewhere nearer Pittsburgh with Mary.

George and Gid had not hesitated to follow him to the crude shelter he had made for himself and his horse in the woods. For hours they had talked and schemed. Gilfillan knew every trail, hill and valley for miles in all directions. He knew where pack horses could make their way through the woods and down to the National Pike with furs stolen on the wilderness road. He knew how they could be caught. Only his desire to expose the real thieves held him in the woods above Wheeling, once he had heard all George had to tell. When they parted, George and Gid had promised to help him.

Three days later, with bang and clatter, Wasser barking and all three drivers shouting to their horses, Weller and George and Gid came to a stop at McKeeb's post. The noise again brought him to the door and he stood as before, his deerskin trousers and jacket a little more frayed, his black hair and beard as shaggy as George remembered.

"Drive into the yard back of the post and take your horses to the stable before the inn's full," he called his eyes taking in the wagons and the two strange wagoners.

No sooner were George and his companions seated in the inn than McKeeb joined them.

"How's Fort Pitt?" It was the same old question.

"You've heard of the Monongahela bridge?" George asked. "We were the first wagoners to cross it."

"No!" The trader sounded incredulous.

"You can expect more wagoners to work between Pittsburgh and the Ohio cities," George predicted confidently, his eyes taking in every object in the room. "My brother Johannes and Lou Ludwig came down about two weeks ago. Did they stop here?"

"Yes, and took loads on into Ohio," McKeeb answered. "They were talking of staying on the National Pike."

"They may change their minds." George spoke with a knowing air. "How far did they go? I want to see Johannes before we go back."

"Yes?" McKeeb asked and waited a moment for George to

say more. When George did not reveal the nature of his business with his brother, McKeeb got up with an air of indifference. Johannes and Ludwig had taken loads to Zanesville, he told them, but where they might go from there he did not know.

Nothing was said about Gilfillan or his daughter; nothing about the message George had left a year ago; nothing about a load of furs for Pittsburgh.

In the days while George and Gid and Weller waited, they became convinced Gilfillan was right about Jennie. There was not a kerchief or a hair to indicate the girl ever had been at McKeeb's post or the adjoining inn. If two unattended ladies had arrived from Pittsburgh only a fortnight before someone would have remarked about it, George was sure. At first he peered too openly perhaps into the bonnets he saw coming toward him on the street, but soon he stopped looking. Unless Mary had money, they could not have paid passage to Wheeling and they were not at Zane's and had not been. It was the only place they could have stayed.

By the third day Gid was restless. With Wasser at their heels he and George were strolling along the wharf, while Weller lazied at the dingy, smoke-filled inn, spinning yarns with other wagoners who had stopped to get a horse shod or a wheel repaired. The broad Ohio glistened cobalt blue, and the late afternoon sun silvered the ice along the bank, reflecting rainbow hues in the occasional floes that eddied and swirled at mid-stream.

"How long will Gilfillan wait?" Gid asked.

The question was worrying George too. He kicked at the levee planks and shook his head. Gilfillan had been annoyed when George insisted he must see Johannes before he started back to Pittsburgh.

"He said he'd watch each morning at daylight so he'd know

when we started," George reminded Gid. "He didn't set any limit to the time."

"But suppose they went on to Cincinnati?" Gid suggested.

They turned from the river and walked toward Zane's Trace in silence. The farmers along the route who built it had done as well as Mordecai Cochran and his Irish Brigade, with all their Union money, George thought.

"We could get loads for Ohio and expect to meet Johannes on his way back instead of idling here," George offered. "If we do that, Gilfillan won't wait. And we promised him."

"Catching the thieves is as important to Gilfillan as letting Johannes know about Grossedawdi," Gid said. "We could leave word for Johannes. . . ."

George did not hear the rest of the sentence. No longer could he put off telling Gid what was on his mind. He took the worn felt hat from his head and wiped it carefully on the arm of his leather jacket, avoiding Gid's eyes. The road was suddenly very cold and quiet, the drilling of the woodpeckers very loud. Behind them the muted noises of Wheeling sounded—the rumbling wheels, the bark of a dog, hoarse voices calling.

"When we see Johannes I'm not going to tell him about Grossedawdi," George finally said. "Johannes should go home, but not because of the share in our inheritance that Pep is giving us now. He should go because it's right."

George heard Gid's gasp of surprise and went on quickly before he was interrupted.

"Johannes is the eldest son, Gid. How can Pep be sure of what's in his heart and why he comes home, unless he goes without knowing of what happened the night he left?"

"But the grays," Gid protested. "Pep told you they were for Johannes. That you should tell him."

George put the hat back on his head deliberately. "I'll not

even tell him about the grays. Not unless he refuses entirely to go home," George insisted.

"And if he does refuse? If he will not go?" Gid's voice was hushed now, cautious and apprehensive.

"The horses are his. That I'll tell him if I must."

George hesitated. Was this the time to tell Gid of the decision he had made? Did Gid surmise that if Johannes would not go home, George must? Did he guess the worry that had harrassed George so long?

Before George could decide whether to say more, Wasser's excited barking demanded attention. The dog jumped up at George, then started running down the Trace. Once he looked back, hesitated and barked again, then raced on.

"It's Johannes!" George declared. "It must be."

They followed Wasser and, turning at a bend in the road, they saw the great grays coming, almost upon them, Ludwig driving behind.

Gid ran ahead of George, shouting eagerly. "Hello, Johannes! Hello!" He did not look back at George but waved to Johannes, and when the horses came alongside he slapped at their flanks and pulled in friendly fashion at Johannes' boot.

"You Gid! You George!" Johannes spoke cheerfully but he looked from one to the other with surprise and uncertainty. "I didn't expect to see you on the National Pike."

"Why not?" Gid asked easily. "We must make money this winter too. What about the Ohio business? Did they feed you well along Zane's road?"

Johannes' forehead furrowed and his long face seemed thinner than when he left home a few weeks ago. Perhaps the question was unfortunate.

"There aren't as many inns as along the Lancaster Road, but we were fed well enough," Johannes replied. "You, now. Have you loads for Ohio, perhaps?"

Gid pulled at Johannes boot again. "Come on off your horse and let George tell you," he said. "I'll take the grays to the inn. You're headed for McKeeb's?"

He pulled Johannes from the saddle horse, laughing and slapping at him. "Come on! You've sat astride that animal long enough."

Johannes had no wish to turn his team over to Gid but he was no match for the big frame and the powerful arms that were pushing him away from the wagon. Gid grabbed the jerk line that had fallen to the ground and in another minute was driving away from George and his brother.

Johannes turned on George. "What's the meaning of this?" he demanded. "What has the fellow got on his mind, jerking me off my horse?"

Johannes was puzzled and scowling in anger. His dark eyes flashed when he faced George and the look he cast in Gid's direction was far from friendly.

"Let's not be quarreling when Ludwig comes along," George said as quietly as he could. "There's something I've got to talk to you about and Gid knew the inn is no place, with every curious driver watching and listening."

There was logic in the explanation and Johannes' nod acknowledged it. They walked to a fallen log and sat down, waiting silently until Ludwig, who had heard the shouting, passed them with a wave of his whip and a noisy greeting.

"Now, George, let's hear it," Johannes demanded. "What's so important that this blacksmith must pull me off my horse before I can get to the inn?"

George hesitated. He mustn't make an angry retort now. Perhaps Gid had acted too impetuously, although George understood his intention.

"Gid is eager to get started back to Pittsburgh but I insisted we stay until I could talk to you," George began. "We heard you and Lou were going to haul on the National Pike instead of the Philadelphia road. I might not see you again this winter."

"And what of that?" Johannes asked.

"Johannes, we must decide what we're to do after this winter," George explained. "Sensibly, and not with misunderstanding between us."

"Then decide for yourself, and as you wish," Johannes said coldly. "Why should you consult me? Whatever you want at home, it's yours. It always has been, all our lives. You're the Dutchman, not I."

George gripped his knees with both hands. Once more he saw Pep's face; once more he reminded himself of Pep's admonition. Unreasonable as Johannes was, he could see a little better how his brother felt—had always felt. When he spoke he was surprised at the evenness of his voice.

"No more mine than yours, Johannes," he said quietly. "Perhaps not as much, if you understood Pep better. If you thought more of Pep and less about you and me."

George felt Johannes stiffen, sitting there beside him.

"What I do after this winter depends on you," George pressed. "So what is it you plan? A farm in Ohio?"

"Ohio . . . hauling with Ludwig . . . what does it matter?" Johannes' voice was bitter.

"It matters. To Pep, who's expecting you to come home. And to me, because I don't want to go back to the valley, but must if you will not."

"What?" Johannes looked his amazement.

"So what is it you plan to do, Johannes?" George urged. "You can see that I must know."

Johannes drew a long breath and looked away from George. Finally he answered.

"I'd planned to ask Pep if he would sell the grays when I

take them back in the spring. Ludwig will buy them and he'd have me haul with him. But he'll buy others if Pep won't sell. I'd planned to haul until I'd saved enough to try for a farm in Ohio."

George scarcely heard Johannes' last words. The weight of a mountain rolled off his shoulders when Johannes said he would take the horses home. With relief came humiliation too. Why had he doubted Johannes' honesty? Pep had not doubted. "Put yourself in Johannes' place," Pep had said, and George had tried. Humbly, now, he tried again.

"But if I go, Johannes? Is Ohio better for you than Lancaster County? And Pep who's expecting you back? Elizabeth, who's waiting?"

Johannes did not answer at once. When he did there was no anger or rancor in his words or tone.

"Leaving as I did, I thought Pep and August Yoder would make other plans than those they decided upon so long ago. I thought it was what you wanted, all of you."

"But what I want is to set up my own wagon shop in Pittsburgh with Gid," George told his brother. "When I told Pep, he understood. Since we were children he's known you were the farmer, I the wagonmaker."

"And it's Pittsburgh you want? And Pep agreed?" Johannes spoke as though he could not believe it.

"Everyone agreed. All are expecting you to take your rightful place at home."

Johannes did not look at George. For a moment he sat, elbows on his knees and head in his hands, and George could not see his face.

"Does Pep know I've been thinking of getting my own farm?" Johannes asked without looking up.

"Not from me," George assured him. "It was bad enough

to admit I wanted to go. I couldn't tell him you might leave him too. And both of us can't."

A lean and muscular hand reached out gropingly and found Wasser's head. The dog moved closer, resting against Johannes' leg.

"I never wanted to go, George." It was almost a sob.

For a long time they sat on the log without talking but no words were needed between them at last. When Johannes finally asked of George's plans and when he would start back for Pittsburgh, George found himself telling Johannes everything—all about the fur robberies and Ramsay's suspicions, and Gilfillan and the promise he and Gid had made to help Jennie's father track down the thieves.

Johannes listened intently. "You've actually seen this man who says he's Gilfillan? Clearly and in the daylight?"

"Yes, in the woods near the inn."

"And his face? It didn't bear scars from Sall's teeth?"

George had completely forgotten the scars.

"Neither his face nor McKeeb's!" George said. "Ramsay thought the robber would be Gilfillan and I, McKeeb. Neither of those two got nipped by Sall."

"The one who did is the one who not only got the furs but who knows all," Johannes said thoughtfully. "How would Gilfillan catch him?"

George sketched the plan briefly. He and Gid and Weller would take furs when they left Wheeling. Gilfillan, hiding in the woods near town, would know when they started. If any attempt was made to rob, the wagoners were not to offer resistance. Gilfillan, armed and waiting where the trail came through to the Pike, would catch the thieves with the furs in their possession.

"A good plan if Gilfillan is honest as you believe him to be,"

Johannes said. "If not, you'll lose Ramsay's furs again and perhaps get hurt in the bargain."

It had not occurred to George to question Gilfillan's honesty.

"Gid believed him too," George insisted. "We were to save ourselves and our horses, at any cost. Wasser too. He's to ride in Gid's wagon and not run behind mine as last time."

But Johannes had raised a doubt. The plan could deliver the furs to the highwaymen without a hand raised in opposition. George and Gid could have been wrong in their judgment of the tall, angular Scot.

"Ludwig knows that National Pike and where the trails come in," Johannes said thoughtfully. "Our loads must be delivered in Cumberland. We could have wheel trouble at just the point where the trail comes in, George."

"You. . . . You could be waiting there? You think Ludwig would?"

"Ludwig's about as gentle and pretty as a porcupine I know," Johannes said. "But he's a good man to have along if there's trouble on the road."

It was more than George would have asked; more than he could believe. He could only look at Johannes in silent gratitude.

18

"ISS GOOT"

"A picayunne says it's Ludwig!"

"My levy's on Weller, the big brute!"

"A reel on Lou! A reel on that ox of a man!"

It wasn't the first time George had heard bets laid nor was he surprised at the names being shouted by the excitement-hungry, gambling wagoners when he and Johannes drew near McKeeb's. The noise and hubbub were coming from the fenced-in yard behind the trading post.

"I wonder what they're up to," Johannes questioned. "Those two have been rivals for years."

George was sure of it. "I've not forgotten that Weller offered to top any price for the grays," he recalled. "There may be more to it now than proving who can lift the greatest weight, though."

Johannes looked at George quickly.

"There's a feeling in Pittsburgh that Pennsylvania wagoners should bring their loads back home, not to Cumberland and Baltimore," George explained. "Pennsylvania had to build its own roads and fight alone to keep commerce with the west coming through to Pittsburgh and Philadelphia."

"I'd heard the talk," Johannes admitted. "If I hadn't been wanting money for a farm. . . . But the loads Ludwig and I have now are to be delivered in Cumberland. They can't change this trip with a wager."

"There shouldn't be any question of that," George agreed but he was wondering what rash boasts Weller and Lou might have made and what was at stake. Weller would have been proud indeed to return to Pittsburgh with Ludwig and Johannes driving behind, but if he did there would be no one on the National Pike waiting to do battle with the robbers when they came out of the woods with the stolen furs.

The setting sun threw a long shadow from the high board wall across wagons and men when George entered the yard, and at first he could see neither Weller nor Ludwig. The drivers were crouched on their knees peering under Weller's wagon and among them George at last saw Weller himself.

"Give it a lift now, Lou!" one man called.

"Push up from your buttocks!"

Then George saw Ludwig, flat on his back beneath Weller's empty wagon, arms and legs reaching upward to the bottom boards.

"Lift it, Lou. My money's on you!"

"Johannes!" George gasped. "Weller's wagon weighs 3,000 pounds at least."

Johannes had dropped to his knees and his face was tense. Whatever the stake, his concern was for Ludwig. Cautiously George looked at Weller. The powerful Dutchman was on his hands and knees beside the wheel nearest Ludwig, his eyes on the ground. Two others were watching with him.

The shouting stopped. Above the heavy breathing of the betters came the gasps of the straining contender, loud and agonized. Three times Lou Ludwig placed hands and feet flat against the wagon bottom and with all his mighty force strove to lift it from the ground. But the wagon stood like the forest from which it came and the iron beneath the forest. Lou Ludwig could not raise it. One final groan and he lowered his legs. Gasping for breath he lay stretched on the ground in defeat.

"Nor can you, Peter Weller!" came in angered defiance from one of Ludwig's supporters. "Let's see you do it!"

Weller rose and waited until Ludwig, breath restored, at last crawled from under the wagon.

"If I do, then you return to the Pennsylvania road?" He was looking Ludwig straight in the face. "You return, ya?"

Ludwig wiped the sweat from his forehead and blinked it out of his eyes.

"After I deliver this load." He was still gasping for breath. "That was the wager."

"That was."

Weller turned his back on the gaping crowd and pulled himself up to his full height. He breathed slowly, deeply, and stretched his arms up toward the top of his wagon. Then he, too, lowered himself, crawled beneath and lay prone on the ground while Ludwig and two others watched the wheel beside him.

George thought he could not breathe at all. Weller must know he could lift his wagon or he would not have made such a wager, but it seemed an impossible feat. More than once George had heard wagoners boast of lifting their wagons but never before had he seen a man attempt the proof.

At last the massive shoulders moved slowly, adjusting for position. Two legs, firm as tree trunks, rose from the ground, feet to the bottom boards. Two arms reached upward. George heard Weller take a deep breath, then another and another. He heard the telling, straining gasps and with the rest pushed forward, nearer to the wheel all were watching. Then came the shout.

"Liewer Gott!"

"He did it!"

"The first try, ya?"

Ludwig stood up and waited until Weller got his breath and crawled from beneath his wagon. "I'll see you at Ramsay's," was all he said.

Weller did not try to hide his satisfaction. "I could always beat you, Lou Ludwig! Now let's see what the inn provides."

George turned from the contenders to find McKeeb watching, silently, at the back of the crowd. Now was the time to talk to the trader while the others were toasting the victor at the inn. He walked to the post and McKeeb followed him inside. It was almost dark and the place was rancid with the smell of tobacco leaves, cotton and raw furs. McKeeb fumbled to light a lantern.

"Ramsay will pay for another load of furs, McKeeb," George said quietly. "Only this time I must know which wagon they're in and how they're packed."

The flickering light cast eerie shadows about the crowded room and seemed to darken the trader's heavy beard.

"Ramsay's had a lot of trouble," McKeeb began. "I've always followed his instructions . . ." The dark eyes glanced at George and looked away.

"I know," George said. "Kline had the instructions last time. I have them now."

"The furs were put in your wagon at Ramsay's word. The others were to guard you." McKeeb looked at George again as though seeking an indication that no blame was attached to him.

"I know," George repeated. "I want them in my wagon this time, too."

The trader hesitated. "You're prepared?"

"With a good Conestoga rifle left over from the last trip." If George's suspicions were correct, McKeeb knew he had the rifle. This was as Ramsay had schemed and Gilfillan had agreed. McKeeb might know he was suspected but the wagoners were not to indicate they mistrusted him.

They loaded before daylight the next morning and with Gid driving first, George and Weller following, the long haul back to Pittsburgh started. Before they came to the tortuous, narrow road that curved sharply over ledges and around wooded hills, Wasser was hidden safely in Gid's wagon where he could not interfere with the robbery they all waited for. It was impossible now for the wagoners always to keep in sight of one another. Only the bells could tell them all was well.

"If you do bring out furs, arrange a signal with the bells," Ramsay had advised. "George has the rifle and he may as well carry it in sight, for they know he has it. You others have an iron tip on your whips. If anyone is molested, contrive to strike the heavy bells on the off wheel horse. That way, even if the robbers let the horses go on and the bells keep up their clatter, you should be able to warn one another and protect each other."

George recalled the night they had sat in Ramsay's kitchen and made the plan. "I'd rather you found Gilfillan and brought him back, than the furs," Ramsay had said. Even Ramsay did not expect them to return with both. Now if all went as planned, George knew he should soon be attacked. He would strike the harness bell before he dropped the rifle as the thieves would order. Gid ahead and Weller behind would close in slowly, allowing the pair to get away with enough of Ramsay's furs for Gilfillan to furnish evidence.

He held the rifle across the shoulders of his saddle horse, its slate-black barrel ready to strike against the bells. He told himself there was no danger but he was re-living the day a year ago when a man had sprung from behind a tree to grab Barney's reins—the man who had struggled with him in the snow until Sall's vicious teeth had driven him off. He tried not to glance up from the rifle and jerk line, but his apprehensive eyes kept looking to the dark trees that lined the road, their skeleton branches clasping bony hands overhead.

Slowly, step by deliberate step, the horses crawled along the uphill road. Ahead, Gid's bells chimed evenly, rhythmically; from behind came the reassuring notes of Weller's heavier bells. Another curve, over another hill. At each bend George fairly held his breath and waited. Was this the clump of trees that hid the robbers from view a year ago? Once more he glanced at the banks of snow that rolled from the rutted road back into the forest. The occasional tracks of a rabbit, or perhaps a wolf, were all he saw.

George had been so certain his wagon would be robbed that he could scarcely believe he was leaving the danger point behind. Could McKeeb possibly have believed this load should go through unmolested because George had a gun? The robbers would both have guns too. Could Johannes and Ludwig have talked and been overheard? What of Gilfillan, at the place where the trail met the National Pike, if no robbers came through to where he lay in wait for them?

A few more miles and George would see Gid driving out into the straight open stretch where a robbery was much less likely. He was beginning to feel cheated—more disappointed than relieved—when an angry shout from behind startled him.

"Get out! Get out, you swine!"

Weller was screaming curses.

George stopped the horses with a quick jerk and the next instant was off Bill's back and running, gun in hand, toward Weller. What could have happened? The furs were on his wagon. Didn't the robbers know? Or had the furs been moved to Weller's wagon? They had loaded their wagons themselves early yesterday morning, but while they were eating breakfast a change could have been made. It must have been!

Weller was still shouting imprecations when George stumbled around the hillside that separated them. Only the woods echoed the Dutchman's shouts, and he stood behind his wagon waving his arms and stomping his feet in rage. In the snow at his feet lay two bags, lashed together as George remembered them, so they would hang over a horse's back.

"What happened?" George gasped. "How..."

He followed Weller's eyes to the back of the wagon and the big white top now gaping open, the ends flapping in the cold wind. Weller pulled his hat from his head and hurled it into the snow.

"I should have known! Stupid fool, me!"

"Known what?" George asked. "What happened?"

"The horses!" Weller was choking with wrath and almost blue in the face. "They began shaking their heads and acting skittish a mile back, but I didn't see or hear a thing until a minute ago. Then one of them that was behind let out a whinner."

"You mean the robbers' horses? The thieves had sneaked up behind, and you the last one in the wagon team?"

Weller nodded. "The devils knew their horse had given

them away. They'd been still as death until then, tossing bags out of my wagon and loading them onto their pack horses. They had two animals. . . ." He pointed to the rutted road that wound down and around out of sight. "When their horse let out that snort they were noisy enough with their orders. 'Keep yer mouth shet'," he mimicked. " 'Keep yer butt on yer horse an' keep movin.' "

"And how you obeyed!" George observed. "You might have got shot for your defiance. Beside, we want them to get away with the furs."

Weller's honest mouth fell open. "But they were to have taken them from your wagon . . . a few bags only, before I came along . . ."

"You weren't supposed to have furs," George reminded him. "Those furs must have been transferred from my wagon to yours while we were eating breakfast at McKeeb's. Wasser would have let out a yelp if the load had been touched at night since we left Wheeling."

Around the bend Gid came running while George and Weller pieced together what had happened.

"Maybe we were outsmarted," George admitted after he had told Gid what had taken place. "This isn't the way we'd planned it, but we probably should have known it wouldn't happen that way. It's not going to be the way they planned it when they get to the Pike, either!"

"No," Weller agreed. "Gilfillan will be waiting."

"Gilfillan and Johannes and Ludwig too," George told them.

"Ludwig?" Weller stared at him in surprise.

"Johannes?" Gid's eyes were shining and he clapped George on the shoulder.

"I couldn't let you know before," George explained.

"There was always someone around to listen. But when I told Johannes what we had to do on this trip. . . ."

They were both looking at George, each with his own question in mind.

"Johannes won't be wagoning on the National Pike either, Weller," George said proudly. Then, because it was easier to tell it to Weller than to face Gid's penetrating eyes, George went on. "He's going home to the farm in the spring, for Pep needs him and the grays there."

George turned away from them to start back to his wagon. He had said enough. This was all they needed to know. But even as he thought it, he could feel the look that passed between his friends and could sense Gid's silent rejoicing while they walked back to their wagons, side by side.

"Iss goot," Weller called to him. "Everything. Very goot!"

19

BLUEPRINT FOR TOMORROW

They waited at the inn near the spot where they first met Gilfillan, for that was as they had agreed. There wasn't any question that the thieves with their loaded packhorses would be caught, and no real doubt in George's mind that Gilfillan would be bringing them back with him to face Ramsay and the punishment they deserved. He fretted though while he sat in the dismal inn playing loo, or walking down the road impatiently, trying to figure the time it would take the robbers to get to the Pike, and the time to allow Gilfillan to bring them back.

Now he worried about Jennie again. Where was he to start looking for her when he reached Pittsburgh? Once she had gone to school. That was a starting point. Her teachers would know who her friends had been and where they lived. Mary must have friends and relatives too. Surely Ramsay would have made some inquiries while he was on this trip to Wheeling. He might have found some clue, if he had not found her.

George felt more free to talk to Gid now that he had nothing to conceal and their plans were no longer in jeopardy. It was good to be able to talk freely of Johannes, since it was certain he would return home to Pep and Elizabeth.

"I keep trying to think what Bevy would do if she had been in the situation Jennie was in," George said while the two groomed their horses.

"She would have gone to Anna," Gid said promptly. "Even though Bevy and Anna had not seen each other for a long time, they could depend upon each other. Somewhere in Pittsburgh Jennie must have such a friend. Tell me again how she looks."

So George described the mass of copper curls, the soft oval of her face, the green eyes that were more beautiful every time he thought of them. It was like Gid to understand how much he wanted to talk of Jennie. Gid probably was thinking of Anna while George talked.

They were planning what to do first after they reached Pittsburgh when George spied the chain of men and animals that turned out to be Gilfillan's. One man on foot led the horses, and the trapped, gun in hand, rode in the rear. Both pack horses were limping. Silently George and Gid stood in the yard waiting. There should have been two men with Gilfillan.

"Look!" Gid exclaimed, gesturing toward the man who reached them first, but George was already looking. Two ugly scars across the fellow's chin told the story. Otherwise the face was heavily bearded beneath the fur cap pulled low to cover forehead and ears. The robber scarcely glanced at George and Gid, but leaned heavily against one of the loaded animals. He was older than George would have thought, from his remembrance of their first encounter.

They were a weary, bedraggled sight, men and animals.

Gilfillan fairly pulled himself from his horse and shaking his head, handed the gun to George.

"It'll be up to one of you to watch him tonight," he said. "I've had no sleep since I got them—and thanks to your brother that I got them both."

"Both?" George questioned. Where was the other?

Gilfillan did not answer but started for the inn. "Don't let him out of your sight," he warned.

"I'll take care of the horses," Gid offered. "The furs we'll load back onto Weller's wagon, and put Wasser there to guard them. Send Weller out to help me, George."

George motioned the robber ahead of him and together they followed Gilfillan into the inn. There was so much George wanted to know that he could scarcely refrain from questioning the trapper, but once inside Gilfillan dropped into a chair, rested his head on the table, and almost instantly was snoring. George turned to the man beside him.

"Sit down," he directed. "What's your name?"

"Mel Brown." The man took the chair George indicated and began pulling off his boots. The stockings he wore were ragged and filthy and his feet bleeding.

"Who's the other one, and where is he?" George demanded.

"Yer brother an' the other wagoner had the law with 'em an' they took him," the man replied. Then, with evident satisfaction, "He's Dave McKeeb's brother Dan."

"What?"

"Oh, I don't mind tellin' ye," Mel Brown said almost eagerly. "A warm jail's goin' to look real good to me. Specially if there's somethin' to eat beside wild meat, an' mebbe a little soap an' warm water."

"So McKeeb was in on it."

"Dave McKeeb engineered it," Brown volunteered. "What did ye think? How else could we allus know who had furs?

We wuz all makin' out fine until that horse of yern did me in. After that, the McKeebs' took all. I couldn't show this scarred mug of mine anywheres."

He rubbed his swollen feet and winced when he pulled the stockings loose from the bloody scabs.

"Could ye get that devil of a trapper to let me ride one of the nags, after ye get yer furs back in the wagon?" he asked. "I ain't puttin' up no fight. I told the officers everythin' and I'll tell this here Ramsay everythin'. Fer a solid year I've lived in them woods, scared to death of bein' seen. No one to talk to except Dan when he showed up with another job to be worked on. An' him treatin' me like I was a dog, an' takin' all, an' threatenin' to turn me in if I ever showed up in Wheeling. Oh, I've had enough. More'n enough. I didn't put up no fight when Gilfillan come up from behind with his gun. Me? I wuz glad to be caught. Dan, he tried to run fer it and he'd of got away except yer brother an' that big Dutchman an' the officers wuz waitin'."

Mel Brown was anxious to talk. Anxious to be with human beings again. One long year in the woods alone had all but turned his mind. George was almost sorry for him.

"When Gid comes in I'll see what can be done about your feet," George promised. "And you can ride to Pittsburgh. There's no sense in slowing us all down, just to murder you with walking."

So Mel Brown rode to Pittsburgh, his feet bandaged in clean cloth and decent food in his stomach at last. He was the most cheerful one of the lot and completely unconcerned that Gilfillan's gun was pointed at his back. Because the trapper insisted, someone sat propped against the wall of each inn at night, lest he attempt to escape, but not once did the robber rouse himself to even look toward the door.

It was a strange outfit that George led onto the Monongahela bridge late one afternoon just before Christmas. Behind his own shining wagon came Brown riding one pack horse and leading the other, then Gilfillan and his gun. Next was Weller's wagon with Wasser guarding the bags of recovered furs, and last of all, Gid. At the tollgate they stopped to pay their fee—sixty-two cents for each wagon and team. The collector looked them over questioningly, his appraising eyes finally coming back to George.

"Your name isn't Bauman, is it? George Bauman?"

For a moment George stared in surprise. He had never seen this man before.

"Yes. Yes it is. Why?"

"I've a message for George Bauman. Sure you're the one?"

"Ask the others," George suggested. Then, "What message could have been left here for me?"

"You're to see Mr. Wilkins as soon as you've got your load safe at Ramsay's."

Mr. Wilkins! Then he had seen George on that memorable day when he crossed the Monongahela. Mr. Wilkins knew he had made a second trip to Wheeling.

"You know where he lives?" the toll collector asked. "It's a big brick house on Water Street. Him and the new wife from Baltimore that he just married last October."

George knew nothing of Mr. Wilkins' private life, but he would have no trouble finding the house on Water Street.

"He said I was to come right away?" George questioned. He would certainly want to clean up and get into fresh clothing before he presented himself at the banker's front door.

"That's what we were to tell you." The man looked from George to the troupe behind him. "You must know why," he added.

George did not know why but he was anxious to see Mr.

Wilkins and find out. Gid and Weller and Gilfillan could tell Ramsay all he knew. There was only one question George wanted to ask of Ramsay. Had he found Jennie?

"Keep an eye to the horses for me, will you, Gid?" George asked when at last they drove onto the cobblestone paving near the stables. "I think Gilfillan and Brown and I should have a word with Ramsay before the inn's so full of wagoners they're hanging from the rafters." Then with a gesture to the other two he led the way to the inn.

George pushed the door open and stepped aside for Gilfillan and Brown to enter first, then closed it with a noisy bang. This room, so big and clean and fresh with the scent of burning cedar logs, was almost like home to him now. Ramsay, sitting on his high stool near the bar, turned slowly to glance through those squinted eyes at the newcomers. But this time it was different. One look and the quizzical mask was gone. Ramsay was on his feet staring at the three of them—the scarred man, bent and haggard and unkempt; Gilfillan towering above him, gun in hand; George, anxious and worried beside them. One look and Ramsay knew most of the story.

"Robert Gilfillan! Did Jennie get through to you?"

Ramsay's question sent the blood pounding in George's temples. This was what he had been waiting to learn and it was bad news. Ramsay had not found Jennie while he was gone.

He listened to the quick questions and the worried answers and finally turned to Brown.

"Sit down. They'll get around to you in a little while," he said and left the inn. He would take care of his horses, get into fresh clothes, and see what Mr. Wilkins wanted. By the time he had returned, Ramsay and Gilfillan might have figured out where they should turn next, and what must be done.

Lights flickered in the windows and the houses on Water

Street were cheerful in the early dusk. Through some of the windows George could see children playing and Christmas gardens like the gay decorations he used to love each year when Mem and Pep brought them from the attic. He had no trouble finding Mr. Wilkins' house; the first man he asked pointed it out to him. Here, too, windows were brightly lighted and through heavy lace curtains George could see figures moving. It was a fine house, bigger than Grossedawdi's or August Yoder's but not built of stone like the houses George admired at home.

For a moment George hesitated at the entrance. It was near supper time and he wondered if he had been in too great a hurry to respond to Mr. Wilkins' summons. The banker well might be entertaining guests. But he had left word at the toll-gate for George to come as soon as the load was safe at the inn. He lifted the knocker, let it drop, and waited.

A Negro maid in a starched white apron opened the door. George had never seen her but she smiled as though she knew him and stepped aside for him to come in.

"I'm George Bauman. Mr. Wilkins left a message for me to come," George said, hesitating at the door.

"Yes sir. I know. Come right in, sir."

She took him into a room which George thought must be the banker's library, or perhaps his study, for the walls were lined with bookcases and the desk and chairs were massive and made for a man. A huge white oak log crackled cheerfully in the marble fireplace and the high polish of a center table reflected the light from two gleaming brass lamps.

"Let me take your coat and hat and I'll get Mr. Wilkins," the maid said. "Make yourself comfortable here."

George was looking at the fine furniture and the impressive rows of books when the banker came in, his hand extended.

"George! How glad I am that you're back safely. When I

saw you driving onto that bridge I was proud of you indeed, but worried too."

"Worried?" George repeated. "You were worried about me?"

"Sit down," Mr. Wilkins indicated a chair. "You see, George, I knew why you were making that trip to Wheeling and I wasn't sure you'd get back with your bells on, this time." He hesitated. "I guess maybe I have something of a surprise for you. . . . Well, I told you once Pittsburgh needed a good wagon factory, didn't I? That we'd be making wagons here to carry the commerce and traffic to the back country? The West will be conquered by Conestoga wagons, George, and I'm convinced you should be one of the builders. One of the wagonmakers who'll make history, too."

It was quite a speech and George wasn't sure he understood what Mr. Wilkins was trying to tell him. How had he known why George was making the trip to Wheeling? How had he known of the danger? Had Ramsay seen the banker?

"You see, George," he repeated, then there was a knock at the door.

"Yes, Susanne?"

The maid opened the door and once more stepped aside. Mr. Wilkins rose and held out his hand. "Come in, my dear."

It was Jennie Gilfillan who came in.

For a moment George sat dumbfounded and not believing his eyes. Then he was on his feet, walking toward her and repeating her name.

"Jennie! Jennie, were you here all the time? Safe all the time?"

"I thought you'd come to Mr. Wilkins as soon as you got to Pittsburgh," she explained quickly. "I thought perhaps you'd be able to take Mary and me to Wheeling some way . . . or tell us what to do."

"Mary came first, George," Mr. Wilkins took up the story.

"She asked if there was work here she could do for Mrs. Wilkins, and if she could keep Jennie with her until you got here. Mrs. Wilkins did need help and we were glad to have Jennie with us. But we all expected you to come to me as soon as you got here. Instead, you went off to Wheeling without ever coming to the bank. I didn't know why you didn't come."

"Oh, no!" George protested. "I did go to the bank. Twice, but you weren't there."

"You did go to the bank?" Jennie asked. She reached a hand timidly toward him and he held it tightly for a moment. "I told Mary you would. I told Mr. and Mrs. Wilkins too. I was so sure you would...."

She looked up at him as she had the night she first came to his wagon in the bitter cold. George stepped closer to her side.

"She was so sure you'd know what to do that she convinced me my first judgment was right," Mr. Wilkins smiled. "I've even been talking to an old wagonmaker here who could use a young partner. No hurry, of course. You may have other things to do first."

George thought he understood the unasked question. It must be uppermost in Jennie's mind too.

"Jennie, I was so surprised to see you I couldn't think. I almost forgot!" He faced her happily and with both hands on her slender shoulders he held her back so he could look at her. "Your father's at the inn right now with Ramsay. He brought back the furs and the thieves too, and everything's all right."

"George! You found him? You really found my father?" Her voice was choked and her eyes filled with tears. "You promised, and I knew you would."

She turned away and Mr. Wilkins handed her his own kerchief, touching her russet curls with a fatherly hand. Over her head he looked at George questioningly.

"Everything's all right, Jennie," George said and nodded

reassuringly to Mr. Wilkins. "Your father's a trapper you can be proud of. Why, Mr. Wilkins' grandfather was a trapper once, wasn't he? Didn't you tell me?"

"That's right," the banker replied. "In the Ohio country, too."

"And now he's at the inn?" Jennie asked, turning to George again. "Mr. Ramsay'll believe him?"

"Of course he'll believe him," George assured her. "They're probably working out a new partnership business this minute . . . unless they're too worried about you to think of anything else."

"Don't be too hard on the crusty old fellow, Jennie," Mr. Wilkins advised. "Go get your coat and run along with George to the inn. I know how worried those two must be, now that they're together and neither of them has you safe under his wing."

She gave him a grateful glance and ran from the room, and a smile lightened Mr. Wilkins' face while he watched her.

"She's a treasure, George. And loyal to you and to her father. Never doubted either of you for a minute."

George shook his head. "That's more than I could say," he admitted. "There've been times when I doubted both of us."

"But now's not the time for doubts," Mr. Wilkins said sagely. His eyes twinkled when Jennie returned, bundled warmly in coat and plaid scarf, and he walked to the door with them, his arm around Jennie's shoulders.

"You should have a lovely walk this evening," he said looking up at the winter sky, bright with Christmas stars. "Come to the bank tomorrow, George. I want to talk to you again."

They set the time and George shook hands with Mr. Wilkins. Tomorrow they would talk of wagons—the wagons he would build to conquer the great west country. Gid and he would be in business much sooner than they had thought.

He fell into step beside Jennie, shortening his long strides and helping her over the rough and crusted drifts.

"There'll be rejoicing at the inn tonight," he told her. "You've no idea how anxious everyone's been. Ramsay—I don't think you know how much he cared about you."

"Mr. Ramsay?" she questioned.

"Of course. He probably never showed it, but when I got to the inn two weeks after he expected me, and he learned you weren't with me, it was your safety he thought of, above every-thing else."

"Why were you late, George?" she asked. "I heard Johannes saying you would be two days behind him and I waited an-other week. Then another load of furs was robbed and I heard Mr. Ramsay questioning the driver about my father. I couldn't stand it any longer, and that was when I told Mary I was going to see Mr. Wilkins. I thought it would surely be only a few days more and I'd see you. I didn't want you to risk bringing out furs again. I just wanted you to find my father. Why were you delayed?"

He told her about Grossedawdi and the horses that were his now; about Johannes and the grays and the farm at home; about Gid and Anna.

"You can see how everything's going to work out, can't you?" he asked, wondering if she saw it as clearly as he did. "You're going to love Anna, just as Bevy does."

"I wonder if I'll even see her," Jennie said softly. "She won't come on to Pittsburgh until spring, you said. I wonder what my father will do with me, now that he's come at last."

"Why, he'll find a home for you, of course," George said quickly. "He can't take you back to Wheeling, where he lives in the woods following his trap lines. Now there's that house of Mr. Ramsay's where nobody lives any more. What about that? Gid and Anna must have a home here. Me, too, when I finish wagoning this winter and settle down in Pittsburgh. Is the house large enough for two families?"

"It's a very big house," Jennie said soberly. "I think it could be made to do." In the darkness she turned her face shyly away from him.

"Then I think I'll speak to Mr. Ramsay about it," George told her. "After I've had a talk with your father."

He sounded very businesslike but he put his arm around her shoulder and drew her closer to his side. He was sure she knew what he was going to ask of Robert Gilfillan.